my
heart
for
yours

steph campbell & jolene perry

Published by

BCC Books

Cover Art by B Designs

The characters and events portrayed in this book are fictitious. Any similarity to real persons, living or dead is coincidental and not intended by the author.

dedication

To the doctors and nurses of the CICU at Children's Hospital, New Orleans,

who fix hearts far more broken than Tobin & Delia's every single day.

-Steph

To my best friend from middle school – I wish this had been your happy ending.

-Jo

I should have started writing a long time ago. But
everything got mixed up. Confused.
I think I heard this somewhere so it feels like a safe
thing to write for my first real page.
I'm still not sure if I'll have the guts to continue, but
maybe I want to, and maybe that's all that counts.

The sea between opposite shores
Does not know
The sides are opposite
Only that the sides are sides.
The shores know
The sea separates them
When really,
It's the body that binds them.

1

Tobin

"Tobin, how are you feeling son?" I flinch as Pastor Mike claps me on the back.

I force a small smile and a nod. I can't manage much else. *Numb.*

Well, numb alternating with feeling like my insides are being shredded. But who wants to hear that? No one. Not even Pastor Mike. People don't want the truth when they ask how you're doing after you lost your brother.

Shit.

How do you lose your brother? You lose your grandfather, your distant uncle, your dog for Christ's sake. Not your brother. Especially brothers like mine. I want to hate him for what he did. Leaving us. It's not right. He's gone and I'm stuck here in this fucking funeral home, staring at his casket. There's no way out. Not for me, and certainly not for him. The casket is closed. Bolted shut for eternity. No one forced him to be a *Jackass* wannabe, though.

I try to avoid eye contact as I make my way through the foyer. Most of these people are strangers, but I know that they know who *I* am.

When I pass the casket display room, I fight the

small twitch of an inappropriate smile. Eamon once hooked up with a girl in there. Classy, right? That was Eamon, though. He could score anywhere and anytime. He was wild, for sure. He'd stay at Carl's playing pool all night and somehow, make it in to work every morning at the oil refinery by five AM, without fail. Never late. Never sick. Work hard and play hard was his motto.

We had some crazy times, he and I, but it wasn't all like that. He taught me how to fish when I was a kid at Coulee de Salle. It became our meeting place when shit hit the fan when we got older. I wonder if I'll ever be able to go back there. He taught me about women. Well, he'd like to think he did at least. I figured out a few things on my own. He taught me to fight, to defend myself, to stand up for what I believe in, and protect the people that I love. I thanked him for that lesson after that weekend in New Orleans when some guy put his hands on Delia and I had to tear him apart.

He slipped me my first beer and always covered for me when I'd had one too many, or when I'd snuck out to meet up with Delia at the boat launch. Shit, I'd gotten to a point where I'd managed to stop thinking about her everyday. I wish she'd stop invading my thoughts right now. I can't handle that on top of everything else.

Eamon had a completely different side to him too. He showed up for church every Sunday morning, ate supper with us every night and would protect my Mama to the death. It's just that he had that other motto. *"I'm not getting old!"* he'd say and I'd always laugh it off. He was my older brother. Untouchable. I never imagined he actually meant it.

I swear I passed a small kitchen or something earlier. I'm not hungry, but hopefully I'll find some peace and quiet. It takes an immeasurable amount of effort to make it down the dark hallway. I run my fingers along the thick, fabric wallpaper to steady myself. Putting one foot in front of another feels like learning to walk all over again. My body's still working. Heart's still beating. Lungs still moving. But not because I want them to. They do those things on their own, without me even asking. So why didn't they do it for Eamon? How could his body just give up on him like that? Fall apart. It made him seem so fragile, and I don't want to remember him that way. He was the strongest guy I knew. How could he break so easily? It seems like our bodies would be built better. It just doesn't fucking seem real.

I push through the double swinging doors into the kitchenette and immediately regret it. Huddled in the corner, Dad and Mom glance up at me but don't say anything. I contemplate backing out of the room. I guess that'd make me look like a total asshole, though.

My mom's in a wheelchair, not because she's injured, but she's been hooked up to a constant sedative drip since *it* happened. I don't know what's going to happen when the doctors take her off of that thing. Will the grief hit her all at once? Flood over her like she's drowning? Or will she feel numb like I do now? Is she just prolonging the misery of feeling like the rest of us do?

"Hey, Pops, Mom," I say. I kiss her on top of the head before taking a seat at the retro looking laminate table.

"Tell me again, Tobin," Mom says.

I inhale deeply and hold it. Every time I do this lately, I feel like I need to see how long I can hold it. See if I can understand how Eamon must have felt. But I know nothing would make me understand that kind of agony. The fear. Did he know he was taking his last breath when he gasped that last time?

"Tell me, Tobin," Mom repeats. I know what she's asking, and it's exactly why I don't want to answer. She wants me to repeat the story of how I found Eamon. I've been forced to relieve this shit for a week now. I don't know why she wants to hear it again. Maybe because she has the luxury of drugs to keep her from feeling, but it's not fair to me.

"Tobin," Dad says. I glance up and he nods at me, encouraging me on. I can't believe this. *He was my brother!* I want to scream.

I finally let the breath out and feel the relief course through me. Eamon never felt that relief. Maybe I deserve to have to retell this story. At least I get to be alive, right?

"I don't know how it happened, Ma. I only know how I found him. He was out there with Traive and Leslie." I don't tell her that what they were really doing. How stupid he had been. "They said he had his back turned. He must've not heard it somehow. When I got there, the medics were already working on him, Ma. They did everything they could. I'm sorry." This is a lie. There was nothing left to work on. There's a reason for the closed casket.

Mom doesn't respond. She never does. I don't know which is sadder. Mom's emotionless glare or Dad's constant reassurance—like he's doing it for her sake, not to keep himself together. I don't think I've seen either one of them cry yet. I wonder when that will come.

"I need to get some air," I say. No one acknowledges me.

I make my way toward the entrance, weaving through a thick sea of black clothing. It's even more crowded in here than just a few minutes ago.

I know for a fact not all of these people knew Eamon. But small towns like Crawford, Louisiana are like that. Even if you didn't know someone personally, you knew someone who did. You served their coffee on Saturday mornings, or they take the offering at Church on Sundays. When your hometown's main claim to fame is being the "Rice Capital of the World," everyone knows everyone. So that's who is here—*everyone*.

A thin, polished woman walks in. She sticks out immediately in her expensive looking navy dress, shiny bag and shoes that probably cost more than I make in a month. My breath leaves me when I see that her arm is draped around a younger version of herself. That hair, it's pulled back way too tight now, but I'd run my hands through it a thousand times before. That face, now in a layer of makeup that makes her look older than I remember, I'd held it in my calloused hands and kissed those lips goodbye over a year ago. She said she'd never see me again and I'd learned to accept that. She destroyed me, and I'd moved on.

No. Not her. She's not from here anymore. I don't know who that person is anymore.

2

Delia

His light blue eyes hit me just like they always have. They go through me, strip me bare, and form a knot in my stomach that's impossible to ignore. How can just being in the room with someone do this to me? He's just a guy. But as I take in his face, a year older, strained with sadness, he's so much more. I was right to be terrified on the long drive.

What can I possibly do here? Seeing his grief over Eamon makes mine pathetic. No one will feel the loss of his brother more than him. Not his parents, not his brother's friends. Not me. No one. Me being here will probably just make things worse, not better. Or maybe that's my arrogance in thinking I might still have the same kind of effect on him that he has on me.

His hair is the same blond mess that I remember, and his suit cuts perfectly over strong shoulders. I wonder if he tied his own tie tonight. It used to be me that helped him; tried different knots until the frustration wore on his face. Always with a hint of tease, though. Because that was Tobin. I wonder if it still is.

"You okay?" Mom's arm wraps over my shoulder making me jump.

She's had her two Bloody Mary's this morning, a

couple of glasses of wine with lunch, so that should last her a while. At least long enough to get her home for her nightcap. It wasn't until recently that I realized how much she needs just to function.

"Delia?" she asks again.

"I…" *have no words.* Now that my eye contact with Tobin is broken, I feel stupid for the thoughts that took me over. Tobin's just a guy—like a ton of guys. Even as I run those words through my head, trying to convince myself, I know it's a lie. Tobin will never be *just* a guy. Not to me. And he shouldn't be *just a guy* to anyone who meets him or to anyone else that's lucky enough to love him.

My heart's cracking apart all over again because of the way I've missed him. I brush a loose strand of chocolate brown hair off my face, trying to blend it into the rest of my up-do. Forcing my head to not turn back his direction is nearly impossible, but I manage. Being hit with him again might ruin my ability to keep my composure here. Instead my gaze ends up on the casket, reminding me of why I'm here.

Eamon was the wildest, coolest, funnest, most full of life guy I knew. Tobin followed his older brother everywhere, but Tobin's wild stunts didn't hold up the recklessness of his brother. Eamon was truly an adrenaline junkie. We always teased him he'd die young—but I don't think any one of us believed that anything was strong enough to actually kill Eamon.

"*Delia?*"

Mom's hand drops off me as I spin around to see Kelly, a friend from school. How did I let myself lose contact with these people? We'd been close. Really close. But I can't even remember the last time I talked to her.

Our arms are around each other, and I hold onto her like my life depends on it. Mom doesn't know how to hold people like this. She knows how to smile, and pat. Not hold. Loss sweeps through me. Loss of friends, loss of Eamon, and loss of Tobin.

"I know. It's awful, isn't it?" Her arms squeeze even tighter.

"I'm still in shock." And the shock of being home, and the shock that Eamon's gone, and Tobin's here—it all floats around inside me.

She steps back and pulls me away to sit against the wall. The flowers have laid a heavy perfume in the air, but everything else in here is weighted with grief.

"How have you been?" She raises an eyebrow, runs a hair through her thick blonde hair, and takes in my outfit. For the first time in a long time, I feel totally self-conscious about what I'm wearing. It wasn't overdone before we got here. But now that I'm back in town, I realize that a Gucci dress and heels is probably a little much for Crawford. Standards in Washington D.C. are a bit different than they are here.

It's amazing how fast I got used to it. Just over a year. It might as well have been a lifetime for how strange it feels to be here. To be home.

"I…" How have I been? How do I answer? Just driving back into this small town snagged something in me that I thought I'd left behind. That I thought I *wanted* to leave behind.

We drove past Fishers Lake earlier and all I could think of was how much I used to love to swim in that lake. How many times did I jump in, fully clothed, not caring that I'd be soaked until I got home. I can't remember the last time I swam in a lake, or waded in a stream. Not since I left him. Or…here. I meant here. Not since I left *here*.

"You still with me?" Kelly chuckles.

"Barely." I lean back. Or maybe part of me never left.

"I hear ya there."

We sit next to one another, shoulders touching, in silence. People are slowly filing in. The air is still thick, heavy, and hard to breathe.

"Your shoes are outrageous," she whispers.

I glance down at my simple black platform heels. "Thanks." And I tried to dress down for this. My eyes float to Kelly's worn black ballet flats. How did a simple move change so much?

"He's so hot, isn't he?" Kelly gestures with her chin to Tobin who's talking to a friend of his brother. Some guy with a weird name that I can't remember. I haven't been gone that long, and I can't remember.

"Yeah." The word breathes out of me before I can contain it.

"If nothing else, I bet you miss *that* part of Crawford." She grins.

And there's really no way for me to argue about that. I have missed Tobin. It's just that I didn't realize how much until I got here.

I make my way to the bathroom as Mom smiles sympathetically and pats arms; playing catch-up with all the women she hasn't seen in a while. I wonder if she cares, or if she's just so used to being polite that it simply happens. My legs aren't working right, they're shaking with nerves, but I still manage in my heels. If I could have seen a year ahead, would I love the girl I am now or hate her? I pull open the bathroom door knowing I would have hated any version of me that wasn't with Tobin.

My phone beeps in a message. Holy Hell, it's been almost non-stop since I left. I pull it out. *Mercedes*. Of course. She's almost as politically driven as my dad, but graduated with me less than a month ago.

MERC: I know you're busy Delia, but I need the signature page you got in support taking down that awful healthcare bill. I also need your numbers for the picnic next week. The caterer is making me crazy.

There are several problems with this. I never went and got signatures because I don't subscribe to my dad's brand of politics. I have zero signatures, but I can't tell Mercedes that. I'll have to come up with some really creative lie.

I'm on it. I text back, even though that's the last thing I am.

Mercedes was queen at the private school Dad enrolled me in last year, and it took me a while, and a lot of work, but now we're friends. Well. Not friends like Kelly and I were—hangout friends. Mercedes was more like—friends by association. Our fathers are in the same Senate committee. She's the southern girl that helped me shed my accent, or most of it.

I still get a look of disapproval from her when I let something cliché like *y'all* slip out.

"It's not cute, Delia," she says all the time. "It makes you sound like a country hick."

I nod, smile, and play it off, but it stings. Every time. To be honest, I can't even remember what this picnic is for, but her dad forgets she has a spending limit on her credit card when she takes to planning charities or benefits or picnics for young republicans. They're small scale, nothing like what my mom's in the middle of at the children's hospital. "But it's all practice," Mercedes reminds me, "for later."

I don't want there to be a later. I want it to be over.

I want my dad to lose the next election and to come home to Louisiana. Or now that I'm graduated, I want to go to college somewhere that no one knows me, and I don't have to work so hard anymore. Somewhere my dad can't constantly look over my shoulder to tell me all the ways I'm doing everything wrong.

When I step out of the bathroom, a sort of line has formed. Guess the mingling part is over. Now's when I get to touch him, or have to touch him. How many kinds of a wretched girl am I that I'm thinking about a guy, when I'm at a funeral? My feet are suddenly killing me, which is crazy because I can stand in these things all day. I *have* stood in these things all day at fundraisers, and political rallies...

It's such a relief Dad isn't here. He doesn't want me within sight or sound of Tobin LeJeune. Not after what I went through. There are just certain things that my daddy would rather never relive. The mess with Tobin is one of them.

I'm a wreck. Screw *floating* thoughts, they're spinning too fast for me to catch them.

Twelve more people in the line between Tobin and me. I'm not sure how the line got started, or even if it's necessary. Mom's in front of me. Dad's back in D.C. because Congress is in session. He can't be bothered to go to Crawford for a friend's son.

Ten more people. I might puke.

Kelly steps in behind me. "Hey." She rubs her hand up and down my arm. "You look a little green."

"Yeah." And yeah is apparently my official word of the day. Perfect. Dad would be proud that my high-priced private school has made me such an eloquent speaker. Mom either hasn't noticed, or is ignoring how I'm shaking right now.

Six people. My palms are sweaty. How bad would it be if I walked away now? Can I? Do I hug him? I mean, that's what you do, right? Can I survive a hug from him? How do I know what to do? Four people.

Mom's hugging his mom, who's in a wheelchair. It breaks my heart to see her like that. Tobin's mom has always been nothing but warmth and smiles. I can only guess that losing her son has her too exhausted to walk. For the year that Tobin and I were together, they were more my parents than my parents were. I did dishes, and helped with family meals, and the memories are breaking me further. I don't need anything else to miss about this place.

"Delia." Tobin's dad stands stoic, stroking his wife's hair. "You look so grown up and beautiful, as always." His chin quivers a bit as he speaks.

"Thanks." I'm so lame. What do I say to these people? Nothing brings back their son. Nothing could make this more awkward. I reach in for a hug, and he holds me with the same strength as he did before I left town.

"We've missed you, sweetie," he whispers in my ear.

My body nearly slumps in relief and relaxation. "I've missed you too." I tiptoe up to kiss him on the cheek, my heart breaking again that they lost their son.

I hug his mom next, but she feels too fragile for me to hug the way I want to. Instead I pat her back a few times as she dabs at her eyes.

One person between us. Anything like relaxation is gone.

I can't breathe.

His eyes lock with mine again—looking hollow, in pain—it's something I don't ever remember seeing in Tobin's eyes before. It's like he's looking at me, but it almost seems like he's just looking because I'm here. Not for any other reason. Not because he wants to. Because he has to.

No people. I'm here. Staring up at him, my heart trying to push its way out of my chest.

I swallow the ball in my throat so I can speak. "Hi." I suck.

His expression is completely unreadable. Maybe I shouldn't have come. It's torture to be so close and not touch.

I breathe in. He smells the same. How is that possible? And how is it possible for it to still make my knees weak? I step in to give him a hug, but his hand comes in between us.

His *hand*.

Because he doesn't want to do any more than shake. With the girl he's made love to. Whose heart is bursting out of her chest.

I'm trembling in a way that makes me feel like I might fall apart any second. His hand touches mine, and I love the warmth of him. Love the way he feels.

My eyes don't leave his. He has only some idea that he could be a model for Calvin Klein. This is so weird. I'm supposed to be angry. Hurt. Instead I'm in shock that he still makes me feel this way—like we were something special.

His eyes hold nothing but pain and confusion— again, something I'm not used to seeing in Tobin. His mouth opens as if to say something, but nothing comes out.

Right.

Of course.

I really shouldn't have expected anything different. Not even now.

I suck in my disappointment, pull my hand away, and walk quickly for the door. I don't care how hot it is outside. I need air.

And I'm pathetic. It's official. I'm standing outside, in the Louisiana heat, in a black dress, black heels, and panty hose that mom insisted on. I'm taking care of those right now. I walk carefully across the rocky outer parking lot to our car. We weren't here early enough for the small paved portion near the church. As soon as I get to Mom's Jaguar, I open the door, sit, and pull the hose off under my dress.

My phone buzzes in my pocket. Again.

WESTON

Okay. I shouldn't need to take a breath before talking to my own *boyfriend*.

"Delia. How is it?" he asks.

His voice is so…like it always is. Tidy. Neat. Careful. I can picture him in his khakis and button up, probably in the student government offices at his university or something. There was just enough slouch in him to attract me. Well, and his parents spend a lot of time with my dad, so being with him just sort of happened.

"Delia?"

"Sorry, I just…it's so hot down here. I forgot how hot it gets. Even at night." I start to fan my face with my hand, but to get air conditioning, would mean getting Mom for the keys. I'm not ready to go back inside, or see Tobin again. At least I can hide in the dimming light outside.

He chuckles. "Well, don't you just sound like a little southern girl already."

"Do I?" I clear my throat, and try to drop the sliding way I use my words down here. "Must be the heat."

"Do you know if you'll be back up before next weekend?"

Right. We have plans. Some debate he has for... I don't remember, but should probably know. It's in my phone somewhere. Weston's getting started young.

I stand up, put my shoes back on, already feeling loads lighter without hose. The church is at the end of Main Street, and a week doesn't seem like enough time to even get started if I want to actually catch up down here.

"Delia? If I caught you at a bad time, you can just call me back." Weston. Concerned. And me, still trying to catch my breath from a handshake.

"It's just hot. And Eamon was a good friend. Being here makes it all the more real." I lean against the side of the car. I still can't believe he's gone. Can't believe Tobin lost his *brother*.

"I can home down there, Delia. You know I would."

"This is a busy week for you." I shake my head, even though he can't see me.

"I'd do it for *you*."

If we were sitting together, he'd have his hands clasped together in front of him, his elbows would be on his knees, and his expression would be very genuine. Weston's polite and caring almost to a fault. But I know he's watching out for me. He'd never pull any crazy stunts, or get me into trouble or beg me to sneak out, or make any ridiculous bargains for pieces of clothing. Skinny-dipping is something I can't even imagine with someone like Weston.

But those are all the reasons I like him.

"I know you'd do it for me. Thanks." I clear my throat again in an attempt to lessen my accent. "Um…thank you."

"You call me, anytime, okay? It'll make me feel better about being stuck way up here."

"Okay." My body's still on edge, but it shouldn't be. Weston cares. He'll come down if I ask and not want anything childish in return for the trip. Unlike some people I know who always want something. Something for everything. Always a trade.

Your shirt for mine, Delia. Come on. You know you want to. Tobin's expression is clear as day. Waist deep in water, his shirt half off, hoping to get mine.

He did.

And a lot more.

"I love you, Delia." Weston's voice snaps me back to the present.

"Love you, too."

I hang up my phone with no idea of why I wanted to be here. Maybe I don't want to be. Maybe just seeing

Tobin again has mixed everything up. I've been doing good in D.C.—steady boyfriend, no more stupid games. Still, I miss it here way more than I've let myself since I left. But life isn't easy, right? Decisions aren't always easy. Sometimes we just have to do what moves us forward.

3

Tobin

What the fuck was that? A handshake? Shit. I contemplate pulling her in for a hug, but she spins on her heels and walks away before I can give it any serious thought.

I had watched her get closer and closer, running lines through my head, but nothing seemed right. The problem is that I still don't know if I'm more hurt, mad, or in shock at seeing her again.

Still, what does she expect showing up here after not so much as a text for over a year? What am I supposed to do? I can barely see her head through the crowd as she makes her way out the front door. I should follow her.

What am I saying? I can't follow her. There are at least fifty more people in line here.

I'm struck by how much this situation reminds me of the first time I saw Delia. She was so close, but so untouchable even back then– before she was Delia Gentry, daughter of a U.S. Senator. It was at a bonfire at Nelson's. I watched her from across the flames all night even though I was there with someone else. I couldn't keep my eyes off of her. Not until Eamon came and talked some sense into me.

"You don't wanna mess around with her, trust me brother. I know her type. She'll be wanting you to settle down in a week. Not like her daddy would approve of you, anyway," he'd said, motioning toward that carefree face. "That's Delia Gentry, Randy Gentry's daughter."

Of course she was. She looked familiar. I'd seen her on TV when her dad was running for town Mayor. Eamon was right. He usually was. I should've stayed away. Still, I don't think anyone could have predicted what would happen with us. With any of us.

I tried to listen to Eamon. I really did. I left with Callie that night, which wasn't exactly a bad thing; she had the nicest tits at the party. But I couldn't stop thinking about that gorgeous girl across the camp fire. No matter what Eamon said, I couldn't stay away from her for long.

I bide my time until the line draws to a close, jiggling the coins in my pocket nervously until I've shaken the last strangers hand. The last time I talked to Delia, she said I'd never see her again. She hung up on me and called me every swear word that sweet Southern girls aren't supposed to say. What the hell was she thinking showing up here today of all days?

I saw Mrs. Gentry step out about thirty minutes ago, so I know that the odds of Delia being here are slim to none. Still, I've got to try to find her. To say what, I don't know.

I'm angry at her for leaving. For not talking to me or returning my calls. And for showing up at my brother's wake unannounced. But the point is, she's here. Or she was. And I shouldn't give a shit. But I do.

I push the heavy door open and the hot, sticky night air hits me. She's there, leaning against her mom's black Jaguar, smoothing her hair down and replacing pins in it. Like anyone here gives a shit what her hair looks like. She wasn't a mirage. She really is back in town.

The sound of the gravel under my dress shoes reminds me of the night Eamon died. The crunch of it under my feet as I ran toward him. Or what was left of him.

Delia glances up without smiling.

"Hey," she says meekly. The sound of her voice again nearly breaks me.

When she left, it was like someone had ripped my heart out, crumbled it up like a flimsy piece of loose leaf paper and crammed it back into my chest. It somehow managed to work, but it would never feel the same.

"Hey, D. You're still here," I say, stupidly stating the obvious.

All of the snide remarks I'd worked around in my mind as I walked out here are gone. I'm supposed to be mad. Pissed. Not broken. Not wanting to stand here and talk.

"Yep. Mom and I," she says. She motions to the front seat of the car. I can see her mother's head through the deeply tinted glass, talking on the phone. Delia stares down at her tiny hands. I can't help but stare at them too, remembering what it felt like to hold them. How they disappeared in my grasp. How somehow, holding her tiny hand made *me* feel safer, even stronger. I doubt that touching them would still have the same effect, not after how we left things with one another.

"I'm so sorry, Tobin," she says. She looks up at me, her eyes are glassy and she's biting on her bottom lip. She looks so delicate.

I nod. I don't know what to say to her. My brother is dead. I want to scream. *I can't deal with you right now.*

"Listen, I think Mom is ready to take off. She's in the middle of planning for this big...never mind, it doesn't matter." Her eyes dart around the parking lot, to the trees, the gravel, the one flickering lamp and its cloud of mosquitoes. Everywhere but at me. "Anyway, we're in town for the weekend, though. If you need something, you know how to get a hold of me."

"Will you actually answer if I call?" I ask.

"What do you mean?"

I let out a dry scoff.

"I mean, because my brother died you'll pick up the phone now?"

"Tobin..." She shakes her head. "Just, call if you need."

She smiles a polite, forced smile and makes her way around to the passenger side of the car. I should open the door for her. *No!* No I should turn around and walk away. Shit, what am I doing?

"Delia," I call as she climbs into the car. I'm not sure what happened to being angry. I'm not sure if it's the fragile was she looks, or her tiny hands, or just her, but I can't let her just get in and drive away.

Her head pops up over the roof of the vehicle. It reminds me of a damn meerkat from one of those nature shows. Everything about this girl still gets to me. That alone should keep my anger at her rolling because that would probably beat the shit out of what I'm feeling right now. Losing Eamon shredded me, but seeing Delia again has added weight. Weight I really need to let go.

"If you want, we could go and grab some coffee or something. I can drive you home later," I say.

She reaches up and pulls on the tips of her bangs like she always does when she is nervously contemplating something before peeking inside the car to talk to her mom.

She leans back out, pulls the pins from her hair and lets it drop. God, I loved that hair.

I remember how many nights she'd snuck out to spend with me. How many times I fell asleep next to her, burying my face in that hair, tangling my fingers in the loose waves.

She shouldn't be affecting me like this. Not after all we've been through. Not after all she did.

I stand in the parking lot staring at my feet, wondering if my brother is screaming at me to stay away again from wherever he is when she rounds the side of the car and her mouth pulls into a soft smile.

4
Delia

One year ago I wouldn't have been able to manage a flat sidewalk in these shoes. Not anymore. Even the gravel doesn't slow me down, but I do worry what it'll do to the leather. I can't believe Mom didn't give me any more than a wave when I asked if I could go with Tobin. He's not exactly high on her list, or maybe she has more going on than I think she does. Or maybe she doesn't hate Tobin the same way that Dad does.

Tobin and I walk in slow silence to his car. Why am I doing this? Why did he ask? Why did I say yes? I'd decided when I left that it would be better if he hated me, easier for both of us.

Going somewhere with Tobin does not work with that plan. At all. As usual, I'm weak and can't follow through.

I catch his eyes again, and it's like the first night I really noticed him, only there's so much between us now that it's way scarier to let him look in my eyes. Will he see what a complete fake I've become? Will he suddenly know I lied to protect him, so he'd be angry instead of hurt?

The night he first actually noticed me, we were at Nelson's bonfire party—one of many. I wasn't quite a junior, and he was going to be a senior that year.

Tobin was with…I don't remember. Some girl with huge boobs, which is probably why he was there with her.

Every girl knew who the LeJeune boys were. Every girl also knew to stay away from them. Except for the line of girls waiting for their turn. And the LeJeune boys were ready to give them all a turn. Eamon especially.

I watched Tobin all night. I know he watched me, but I was careful. I didn't really think anything would actually happen between us. It's hard to wrap my mind around how wrong I was.

He opens the door of the same old Ford pick-up truck that he was always working on and perfecting.

"She looks good." I touch the door before climbing in.

"Uh…thanks." He rubs a hand over his blond hair, leaving it ruffed up in all the right places.

This is so awkward. His eyes are the same. His voice is the same. It's the sameness, and the newness and the differences and all the stuff between us—the good, the bad, the horrible and the selfish. The last two were mostly me. Then came the anger part—that was mostly him. And now? Now I'm just a girl here probably messing with his head in a way he doesn't deserve. The thing is that I don't even know what I want from him. Is there any chance of us even being friends?

Being away from home allowed me to not think about Tobin. About how in the end it was almost like we tried to destroy each other.

It still amazes me late at night when I let myself think about it. Like grandma said all the time—*you make love with the same passion that you make war*—or something like that. At any rate, that was definitely true for Tobin and me.

Every building in this town looks like the trees want to swallow them up. There's a tint of rust on everything metal, and it's all smaller and more worn than I remember. Even though it's dark out, we don't pass a single vehicle where the driver doesn't pause to wave. And because it's just what you do here, we both give a small wave back without even thinking about it. The truck bumps along on the beat up road. The roots from the magnolia trees that have been here since the beginning of time have waged a war with the asphalt of the road and left it full of craters and lumps. No pretenses here. What you see is what you get. That's one part of Crawford I've really missed.

Crawford passes by fast, even though Tobin's driving slow. His thumb taps the steering wheel to the local station quietly playing in the background. I glance around at the vinyl interior. There are too many memories in this truck.

∽

I lay cradled in Tobin's arms as he leaned his back against the driver's side door.

"What do we do?" I asked still in shock.

My heart pounded so hard. Dad had gotten his senate seat after another Louisiana Senator stepped down. Odd circumstances, but it didn't make my dad any less proud to be there. He was winning the Senate race at the time anyway. All I could think about is how the senate seat he just got ran out in two years, and Dad would be back on the campaign trail rampage.

"We'll be okay, Delia." Tobin's voice didn't have the certainty I wanted, but his hands didn't stop touching me, trying to calm me down.

I pulled his arms more tightly around my waist. "I can't believe I'm moving."

"I know." He kissed my head, but didn't say more. Didn't tell me how we were going to make it better. I started to panic, but breathed in the familiar smell of Tobin and the old truck and relaxed again.

Tobin had never let me down before. I knew he'd take care of everything. I didn't know that night was only the beginning of the mess that would tear us apart.

- - -

Tobin sighs next to me, breaking the memory.

"Sorry," I whisper. "Been a while since I've been home."

"Is this home?" There's almost a hard edge to his voice, but he might just be tired.

Or he might hate me.

I don't know. I don't know where home is. Right now I want home to be in this truck a year and a half ago, but is that just because I'm here? I wipe the tears from my eyes and re-cross my legs.

Tobin's eyes glance down, just briefly, and I can't help but feel good that he still sees me. Notices me. Which, really, shouldn't matter. I don't need him to notice me. Shouldn't want it.

"This is still home."

"You're staying at the house, right?" he asks.

"Where else would we be?" His question doesn't make sense.

"Well, I figured I would have heard if you sold it, but since none of you have been back for so long..." he trails off, and all I can think is how I love his voice. Tobin's always had the best kind of southern accent—the kind that makes everything sound smooth, sexy.

"Busy. Dad's always busy. Mom's busy. I'm—"

"Busy?" He tries to do a Tobin thing and pull up a brow, but there's too much grief on his face for me to buy it.

"Yeah." Busy. I'm insane busy. Showing up at the right places at the right time and planning senior picnics and helping Mom with charity fundraisers, and appearances with Dad, well, and with Weston. His dad's a long-time senator from Tennessee, so Weston has the routine down. I'm starting to have the routine down. All of the crap I'm involved in now wouldn't matter to Tobin at all. He hated the very few political dinners I dragged him to.

"Seeing anyone?" He stares at the road, and his hands tighten.

I nearly answer, *Weston. I'm seeing Weston. I love him. He loves me. We're a good match. He was good to me when I was new. He knows the game with our parents, and helped me learn to play it.* But I can't say any of those things. Instead I open my mouth, not sure what should come out.

"You know what? It doesn't matter." He shakes his head. "Never thought I'd be sharing this truck with you again, Delia."

For a second, I wonder if that means he's shared the truck with some other girl since I left, but just hearing my name from his lips makes me swoon a little. I have got to get my head back together. I'm a mess. And it's still so weird seeing Tobin not only dressed in a suit, but to see him without his brother. "Yeah."

He pulls into the parking lot of the diner and climbs out.

Guess we're going to do this in front of strangers. Whatever *this* is. At least he's not yelling at me. I don't think I could take that. I want to ask him about the times that he called me after I moved. The times that he didn't say anything, just sat on the phone in silence. But I guess it doesn't matter what he was calling for. Even though the caller ID showed the number as Private, I knew it was him. I could tell just by the sound of his breathing, which was familiar after all of the times we stayed on the phone in silence, not knowing what to say, but neither one of us willing to hang up, leading up to the day I left.

The familiar smell of burgers and pie surrounds me as Tobin holds open the door. The large L-shaped diner looks the same. Same dark, cracked vinyl on the booths. Same stools at the long counter. This place reeks of my childhood. I remember coming here for lunch after church every Sunday. Now we have a chef to do all of our cooking for us. That is, on the nights when we're actually home.

"DEAL-YUH GIN-TREE!" Missy pulls me into a hug that shoves her enormous boobs in my face as she laughs and squeezes me a few times. "Lord, girl! I wasn't sure if we'd EVER see you again!!"

Right. We're in Crawford. Thinking I'd get to talk to Tobin in front of *strangers* was a ridiculous thought.

I pull back to see her bleach blonde hair high on her head, pen behind her ear, and gum smacking in her mouth.

She couldn't fit the stereotype of a half-manager/waitress if she tried. She even has the uniform—red with a white apron and collar.

"Hey, Missy." I push my hair back off my face, and

it's the first time that I've seen Tobin smile—at my expense no less. Missy is the beginning and end of most of the gossip that circulates through Crawford, and is always inappropriately affectionate.

"And you." Missy frowns, and Tobin stiffens. I'm sure she's about to say something that'll just make him feel awful. Or maybe just give the guy more sympathy than he'd want right now.

"We're starving." I drag him to a table before Missy can go further, but once we're there, I realize I'm holding Tobin's arm. I'd wanted to touch him earlier, but now that I am, I remember I don't get to touch Tobin anymore, and probably shouldn't want it.

"Sorry." I let go and step back, heart pounding, and still having no idea how I feel about being here, or if I should be.

Missy's greeting someone else who's just come through the door.

"You saved me from Missy's bosoms, I should thank you." And Tobin actually has to hold in a smile, but his eyes are still hollowed out.

I don't know if the overwhelming sadness is because of me, or because of Eamon, but I hate seeing him this way.

My phone buzzes in what has to be the millionth text today. I pull it out as we sit. I start to type a response that'll be vague enough to keep Mercedes off my back, but realize that I'm sitting across from a guy who just lost his brother. I'll call Mercedes later. I'm here for a funeral. I'm sure that'll push at least some of her holier than thou attitude away.

"Sorry," I say as I turn off my phone and set it in my purse.

When was the last time I did that? Just turned it off? It feels good. Better than good.

I rub my hands down the fabric of my dress, and wonder again how I thought it wouldn't be too much. And my heels. Probably part of me forgot, and part of me wanted to show up back here and be looked at. Part of me wanted to look beautiful for Tobin. Like he'd care about something like that right now. Now I just feel a bit stupid, selfish, and petty.

Tobin doesn't seem to be looking at anything in particular. He's in another world right now. One I really shouldn't want to be a part of, but that I feel like he needs rescuing from. I don't know what I expected would happen when I saw Tobin again. Nerves hit me as soon as I left D.C., but I was more worried we'd yell at each other. I didn't expect this…confusion.

5

Tobin

I weigh the salt and pepper shakers in each hand nervously. Girls never made me and Eamon nervous. Making girls sweat was our job. Delia was a completely different story. I don't know what the point of me asking her here was. We don't have anything left to say. There's nothing left between us but a bunch of scars. Whatever used to be is long over. *Buried. Like my brother will soon be.*

"Just coffee," I say to Missy. She can't stop staring at Delia and me—grinning like a giddy fool.

"Same." Delia smiles politely. Polished. Perfect.

"So..." I let my voice trail off, unable to come up with anything to complete the sentence. Missy sets the two stained coffee mugs down and pauses again to smile before leaving us to our awkwardness.

"Look, I'm sorry I showed up without calling," she says.

I toss two packets of sugar toward her, because I know things like that—how many sugars Delia Gentry takes in her coffee. Useless information.

"I was afraid if I did, you'd tell me not to come," she says.

I exhale loudly.

"So why *are* you here? I thought you were never coming back to this hell-hole."

Her head jerks against the back of the booth in surprise.

"Geez, Tobin. I loved Eamon, too." She blinks several times like she does when she is trying to keep the tears from forming and her cheeks redden. She goes back to blowing on the steaming liquid, looking wounded.

"You're right. I'm sorry," I say.

We sit in silence for too long for it to be comfortable. It was stupid to ask her to come with me. Eamon would definitely kick my ass for sitting here right now. I stir my coffee, though it's black and has nothing to mix in, and Delia folds her napkin into pyramids and fans and whatever other fancy shapes she can come up with.

"Is that your best party trick out there in the big city?" I ask with an attempt at a coy smile. Something has to change this awkward mood between us.

"Hardly!" She laughs. "You know my best trick was always... Never mind," she says. The rosy color returns to her cheeks, she has to be thinking what I am—of those nights out at the cabin, just the two of us. *Yeah, I know.*

"Do you remember the first time I met you and Eamon?" Delia asks. She's trying to change the subject.

"He made such a fool out of himself that day, huh?"

She laughs. "True story. Complete and total ass."

I love when she accidentally lets her southern twang slip into the conversation. When she isn't trying so hard to be nothing more than a perfect senator's daughter.

I sit back in the booth, a little more comfortable now, and allow myself to really look at her. I search her face for the girl at the boat launch that Eamon and I met that summer afternoon. It feels like a lifetime ago.

∽

"You'd better slow down," I told Eamon. He looked over his shoulder, grinning like an idiot as the waves lapped up over his jet ski.

"Stop being such a pussy and keep up," he yelled back.

It wasn't that I was afraid, but we'd been drinking and Eamon was sure as shit not paying attention well enough to be going that fast.

I spotted them on the dock at what must have been the same moment that Eamon did, because he took off even faster, pushing the jet ski to its limits. I kept up the best that I could. I was the one with the ice chest full of beer that was tied to the back of jet ski, bobbing behind me. Two girls. Two fucking *gorgeous* girls. Say what you will about the South, but I think we have the market cornered on beautiful women.

Eamon continued full speed toward them. I watched the looks on their faces change. They must've been wondering if he was going to stop. He would. This was typical Eamon. He was most likely just going to wait until the very last second. When I got in close enough to see that one of the girls was Delia, I slowed almost to a stop. Watching her.

Her eyes wide with what should have been terror at the sight of Eamon barreling toward her and her friend on the dock. Instead, there was a hint of something behind them. Something that looked like it was begging for excitement. Daring him to keep coming. And he did.

He tried to veer away at the last second, but misjudged how close he was to the dock. The jet ski hit the edge of the wooden platform at a such a high speed that Eamon went airborne before landing on the wooden planks. When I got to him, I saw that his leg was full of splinters and cuts.

The son of a bitch just laughed, even though Delia's friend was screaming that Eamon had broken her dock.

Even with the feisty look in her eyes, I expected Delia to freak from the blood. Instead, she kneeled beside him and pulled off the tissue paper thin tank top she wore over her bikini top. She used the shirt to dab the blood that was slowly dripping from his cuts.

"Am I going to live?" he joked.

"You're lucky I'm not going to have to pull splinters out of your ass. What the hell was that stunt?" Delia asked him.

"I'm so sorry. We'll fix the dock," I said before Eamon could answer, though I wanted to laugh at her serious tone with Eamon. I couldn't take my eyes off of her. The sun kissed shoulders dotted with tiny freckles. Her eyes were a shade of gray I'd never seen before.

And Jesus Christ that tiny top that left just enough to the imagination and had me wanting to take her right there, that instant. I had seen girls wearing much less, but *this girl* was something else.

She shrugged. "Don't worry about it." Her friend started to protest but the narrowing of Delia's eyes told her to let it go.

"Are you going to be okay to walk? My car isn't far," Delia said. "We really need to get this cleaned up. You should get it checked out at the hospital."

"Bull shit," Eamon said. "I'm going to pass on the hospital, but why don't you lovely ladies let us take you out for a drink?"

"I don't think so," Delia's friend said. Her arms were crossed tightly across her chest in annoyance, which only meant Eamon was going to push even harder to get her to go out with us. The bigger the challenge, the more he'd want her.

44

Delia and I had locked eyes minutes ago and she hadn't released me yet.

"Yeah, we'd better not," she finally said.

I felt myself deflate. I didn't know what else to say, so I decided I'd better just help Eamon up and get us out of there. When I reached down to offer him my hand, she was so close that I could feel the heat radiating off of her sun drenched skin. I would've given my left arm to touch her right then.

"Look, we'll get this fixed up tomorrow," I said. She leaned in. I held my breath.

"Meet me back here after midnight," she whispered.

DOUBLE EDGE

The way you looked at me

Love

Mistrust

The way you sounded to me

Distant

Caring

The way you held me

Horrible

Wonderful

The way you left me

The way I left you

In one way

It's the same

I'll never be Whitman, that's for dang sure.

6

Delia

There's a clatter of voices, and a group of people I know comes in the door of the diner, but already I'm pushing hard to remember names. How does a single year cause near-amnesia? Nelson, Rachel, Kelly… It's amazing how much they've all changed in a year, or maybe that's me. No asking, no questioning—the booth in front of me and behind me are now filled. Tobin's gone silent.

I'm still confused. Is it losing his brother that's making him so stoic? I figured the next time I saw Tobin, he'd chew me a new one. Maybe he doesn't care enough anymore to even be angry. That thought hurts me in a way that it shouldn't. Not for a girl in love with someone else.

"Hey, y'all!" Rachel says. "It's like prom flashback, right? Cause we're all dressed up."

Tobin shifts his weight and looks like he'd love to throw a peppershaker across the room. I want to smack her.

"Oh." She touches Tobin's shoulder from behind him. "I'm sorry. I wasn't thinking. I mean…"

Tobin's face falls. I rub the inside of his calf with my foot under the table, because that's what I've always done when I want to tell him I'm sorry without words.

His head snaps toward me, and my foot drops to the floor as my cheeks heat up.

This is so weird. To be close to him, but *not* close to him. To know that he isn't mine to touch anymore. All of the history that we have, and yet we sit here almost like strangers. All of the little moments that we've shared—the way that he used to smile when I'd kiss that certain spot under his ear, the way he'd trace circles on my bare skin after we'd made love—and I can't even tap his leg?

Rachel gives me an apologetic frown from behind Tobin as she tucks her short, brown hair behind an ear.

Everyone starts asking me questions about living in D.C. and what it's like now that my dad's a senator.

I nod and smile and give the polite answers to questions I've been asked a million times. I've been coached on how to answer. The fake repetition is suffocating and makes me want to scream. Inside, I think I am.

I hate it. That's what I want to say to them. I want to tell them that my dad is now an even bigger ego-maniac than he ever was, if they can believe that. And I thought there was pressure smiling for cameras at the little Louisiana campaign picnics we used to have, but those were nothing. Nothing like the supposed 'informal' barbeques, press releases, and the awful realization that I was lower than low when I started at my new school. No one cared that my dad was a senator.

Everyone's daddy was a politician, a businessman, the owners of places like Costco, shareholders in Neiman Marcus. Delia Gentry was a nobody. I've worked so hard to show people that I *was* somebody, all I can think is that with all that work, I'm still nothing.

The voices around us are louder and the laughter's grating against my nerves.

When I glance at Tobin again, he's still and his eyes are almost pleading. I know I need to get him out.

"I'm tired. Can you take me home?" I figure this time, its okay to tap his leg with my foot under the table.

I open my purse and start to pull out my wallet, but Tobin gives me the usual, *don't even think about it* look. He never once let me pay for anything while we were together, and even in this weird situation we're in now, it doesn't look like he's about to start. I wonder how much of what happened between us was because of his pride...or mine.

He tosses a few bills onto the table and jumps up standing without a word—I'm sure he's as desperate to leave as I am.

All I can think about as we drive is that first night when I invited him to meet me on Becky's dock. And he actually showed up. Something about Tobin made me feel brave. It was that he had that same energy as Eamon, but with a bit more common sense.

He was both dangerous and safe all at once. As I got to know him better, Tobin had the biggest heart of anyone I'd been around. He made me feel…passion. And it's crazy, but something about him still does. The problem with passion is it goes both ways. Love/Hate. The line between those two is a lot thinner than I thought.

I waited on the dock just like I promised I would.

"You came." His smooth voice melted me before he came into the light at the end of the dock.

"I invited you," I said, suddenly feeling braver than I ever had. Something about Tobin made me brave. Made me want to soak up whatever made him and Eamon so in love with everything. So crazy and wild and wanting to take advantage of whatever adventure they could. I'd lived my life so far in fear. In fear of what dad wanted me to be. In fear of becoming like my mom—like a shell of a person instead of an actual person.

"That you did, Delia." My name from his lips hit my stomach, and I patted the dock next to me for him to sit down, even though my hands shook a little at having him so close.

Just like earlier that day, the warmth from him hit me sending goose bumps across my skin. I tried to settle myself and play cool, but Tobin had come, in the middle of the night, to see *me*.

"I brought you a beer, but you might not be a—"

I popped the top and downed nearly half the bottle, hoping to swallow some of my dancing nerves.

"—beer drinking girl." He chuckled as he popped the top off of his.

We sat in silence, the dark heat of the air pressing down on us, our legs dangling off the dock. I took a few more swallows. The beer tasted less horrible than I expected. Maybe that was just because of the company.

"Wanna swim?" he asked.

"What?" I set my bottle down.

"Swim, Delia." He smirked. "People do it in the water."

"My parents might sleep like the dead, but I'm not sure about Becky's." I jerked my head back toward her house. Mostly I'd started to realize that I'd have to strip down there, or before I went back through Becky's window. I knew I should strip before getting wet, but no guy had ever seen me in less than a swimsuit before.

"I can jump into the water without squealing like a girl if you can." The look in his face was pure challenge. Always.

It took every ounce of courage I had in me to strip off my shirt and shorts. I was thankful I'd thought to wear a matching bra and panties and jumped in without a word. Holding my breath to keep the water, my squeals, and my nerves at bay.

Tobin stood on the edge of the dock with his mouth hanging open before frantically pulling off his shorts and T-shirt, nearly falling over before half-tripping and half-jumping off the dock.

- - -

A bump in the road pulls me from my daydream. I'm half-living in the warmth of that memory, and half-mad because Tobin should have been there for me when I needed him. He knew how destroyed I was, there was just a lot we never saw coming.

I was hurt then when he pulled away from me at the worst possible time, and in some ways, as I think about what we could have had, I'm more hurt now—I'm just better at pretending than I ever thought I'd need to be.

Distance in geography doesn't bother me, but distance in relationships? That was the deal-breaker. My body stiffens as I remember more than just what it does to me to be close to him. Because he's not the only one with a reason to be mad here.

Tobin's impossible to read. He should still be angry, but maybe the death of his brother has just covered up everything else. The more I think about how we left things, the angrier I become.

"Why did you say yes when I asked you to go with me?" Tobin asks.

"I don't know." At least that's honest.

He shouldn't have asked me to go anywhere with him, and I shouldn't have come. Why would *either* of us want to be around the other? Frustration starts to roll around inside me.

When Tobin and I finally split, he had his brother around.

I had no one.

"I mean, are you dating…" He pinches his nose between his thumb and first finger. Then clinches his jaw tight. Maybe now's when his anger will come out. "You were with…"

"Weston, yes," I snap. What's with me? "I love Weston," I say, lifting my chin defiantly, I don't even know where this is coming from. The words feel heavy and dry coming out of my mouth, like I may choke on them. I don't know how to explain what Weston and I have to anyone, or even to myself.

For me, right now, it's enough to like hanging out with him, and selfishly, to know that he is physically there for me. Because one thing I learned from Tobin is that sometimes the people you love most let you down simply by not being there. Anxiety over the move I could handle, it was everything else that killed me. *Us.*

7
Tobin

"That's great," I say. The sarcasm hangs heavy in my voice. I can't fight it. I wonder how much of her happiness is genuine and how much is because it's the *right* thing. The *safe* thing. The complete opposite of what she had with me.

"So, what about you? Are you seeing anyone?" she asks. She won't look up from her hands, folded neatly in her lap.

I laugh because it's all I can do. She can't be serious. Screw the daring tough guy image. What happened with us broke me.

"D, let's not even go there." I shake my head and she just nods.

"It's this one coming up here on the right," she says.

"I know which house it is, Delia." I've been here a thousand times. Helped her sneak out. Caught her as she slid out of her window. My hands would glide up the length of her perfect body. She trusted me so implicitly. She knew I'd never let her fall, never let her get hurt. Christ, I've got to stop.

"Why didn't you call me when it happened? With Eamon, I mean," she asks.

She peaks out from under her dark lashes. She has too much makeup on. I want to tell her to wipe all that shit off of her face. You can't even see her. Not the *real* her, anyway. Course, I don't even know who the real Delia Gentry is now, maybe I never did. She was a completely different person with me than she was with everyone else. That daring girl from the boat launch was a secret. Something that only I brought out in her.

I thought it was a good thing, but based on how quickly she moved on, I guess it wasn't who she wanted to be.

"I wasn't really in the frame of mind to go tracking you down, Delia." *Also, I've sort of spent the last year trying to forget you ever existed.* "And you don't really have the greatest track record with answering my calls," I say. The words come out much more harsh than I'd intended, stinging even my tongue, and I can tell by the look on her face she's feeling it too. I don't know what the point of this was. We don't have anything left to say.

It's been a year since I've driven down this road. The houses on this end of Crawford are massive and immaculate. Pristine lawns with sprinklers on timers. Gaudy, illuminated fountains in each of the yards. My noisy, beat up truck doesn't belong here. I stop three houses down from hers, the brakes squeaking and the engine idling rough until I give in and shut it off.

I don't even have to explain.

She shrugs and nods. "Yeah, it's probably better this way."

I stare straight out the windshield, trying to make sense of the night. Trying to think of a way to say good-bye to her. *Again.*

Then I see them. What the fuck is he doing here? Mr. Gentry, looking as pompous and full of hair gel as I remember the asshole. I squint to make sure I'm seeing correctly. The boyfriend. Weston. Here.

"I think you'd better go," I say. Each word is clipped and controlled. Not revealing the rage I feel right now.

She bites her bottom lip and looks confused as she stares out the windshield.

"Okay," she says. "They weren't supposed to be here. I'm so sorry, Tobin." She knows. How could she not?

"Just go, D," I say. I wonder if it sounds like begging. Its how I feel.

She slips down out of the truck, but leans back into the cab, her jaw tight, her eyes fixed on me.

"You have no idea what kind of pressure I'm under, Tobin. You don't know how hard it is out there, being a *senator's daughter.* Being the country girl in D.C."

I can't look at her.

"You left me first," she says.

I want to scream *bullshit*, but instead tighten my grip on the steering wheel, and try not to see the younger version of Delia's dad in the driveway. The guy she'll probably end up marrying—I just hope she doesn't end up like her mother. That I couldn't stand.

"Delia. Just *go*." It's all too much. I shouldn't have invited her out.

She shuts the door quietly. Neither her dad nor his minion looks up, so she must be in the clear. I don't watch her walk away. I don't want to see her touch him. I can't.

I turn around in the middle of the road and head back toward town, pleading with my own brain to block out the memory. Please, please don't let it all come back to me today. But it's too late. I'm right back there in my room with Eamon the afternoon that I knew I'd officially lost Delia.

"You hungry?" Eamon asked. "Let's go into town and get something to eat. I don't want to spend my entire day off sitting here staring at your ugly face."

"Fine. Let me show you something first."

He sighed, but followed me from his room into mine, knowing that there would be something deep-fried in his near future if he just complied.

"All right, sit down," I said, motioning to the chair. I turned my back to him and began digging furiously through my closet. You'd think I could keep track of something so important, but I'd always been the opposite of organized.

"Wait," I said, momentarily halting my search. "Did you just get home? Who were you out with last night?"

"I wasn't out," he clarified, grinning.

"Ah, a little walk of shame action."

"Nothing shameful about it, my brother." Eamon laughed.

I reached inside the pocket of a worn out pair of jeans and produced a small, black velvet box.

"Found it!" I said. The lid made a croaking noise as I opened it proudly. Inside was a thin, gold band inlayed with tiny, pin-prick diamonds. It wasn't much. It wasn't even close to what a girl like Delia deserved, but it was all I could do for now.

I know you're supposed to spend two months salary on a ring. Well, sadly, this is what two months worth of pay at Fontenot's Welding bought. I just hoped it'd be enough for her.

"And with that, ladies and gentlemen, I've lost my appetite," Eamon said.

"Don't be an asshole."

"No, no, no," Eamon said, furiously shaking his head.

"Yes, E! I'm going to ask Delia to marry me!"

"Are you fucking insane?" he asked.

"Nope. I'm so crazy about this girl."

"Look at you, all glassy-eyed and proud. You're so ridiculous," Eamon said.

"Eamon, come on. You know how much I miss her. I can't do this for another year. I need to know she's going to be in my life after her dad is done in D.C. I need her in my life forever."

Eamon was staring off into space as if he were trying to figure out some complicated equation.

"Is this because of what happened before she left? I mean, is it a guilt thing?" he asked. "That's it. That's got to be it."

"That's not it at all," I said, snapping the box shut. I wish he wouldn't bring that up. There's nothing in this world that I feel guiltier about than not being there the way I should have for Delia before she moved. I freaked. Panicked. I was a coward.

But shit, she'd suddenly turned into this crazy, clingy girl that she'd never been before—at the exact time that I'd needed thinking space. It was too much.

"But, why? I really don't understand."

"I don't want to be with anyone else," I said. "She's it. Delia's *it* for me. It's not over guilt. I love her."

Eamon rolled his eyes. I wanted to punch him in the teeth.

"Look, if you're going to be a dick about it, you can just go." I said. I shoved the ring box into my top dresser drawer.

"I don't think I'm being a dick, Tobin, I think I'm being realistic. You're only nineteen for Christ's sake! I know this is the South, bro, but what the hell is the rush?"

"I don't expect you to understand, but it's really pretty damn simple. I don't want the same things as you. I don't want to go out every night searching for a different girl. I just want Delia. I just need you to try to be happy for me. I'm leaving tomorrow. I'm going to drive up to D.C. and surprise her."

"Have you told Mom any of this?" Eamon asked, like I needed permission or something.

"No, not yet. I'll talk to her when she gets home from work. Now, we can go and get some food."

I sat on the edge of my bed to put on my shoes when Eamon said, "Tobin, wait." He left the room for a few seconds, and when he came back, he was holding a folded newspaper.

"Mom and I thought it'd be better not to show you this. But I'm not going to have my brother driving

hundreds of miles to make a fool out of himself. I'm sorry, bro."

He handed me the paper, and all of the air left my lungs. No, all of the air left the entire room. The house.

Maybe the earth.

It was her. At some hoity political event at the state capitol. She'd been close and didn't even tell me. I could've driven out to Baton Rouge to see her. Why wouldn't she tell me?

He was why.

The caption under the photo said it all. Everything I needed to know about why she hadn't been returning my calls as often. Why she sounded so distant. Black and white. Right there. And they'd hid it from me like I was too stupid and weak to understand.

YOUNG LOVE: Louisiana Senator's daughter Delia Gentry and Tennessee Senators son

Weston Martins, pictured here at the Conservative Politics Black Tie Fundraiser in Baton Rouge.

I waited for weeks for her to tell me that it was just some big misunderstanding. That they'd been forced to pose for that photo, smiling, his arm draped intimately around her. But she didn't. And her silence when I called only further confirmed what I already knew. There was no mystery here. Nothing to figure out. The only thing to wonder was how I'd deluded myself into believing that I was ever good enough for Delia Gentry to love.

TO MAKE YOU HATE ME

The impossible task
Wasn't as hard
As I'd hoped

8

Delia

Weston. Here. In Crawford. With my *dad*—the guy who was too busy to come. It's so like Weston to swoop in and rescue the girl when she's down. I should be thrilled, but I don't know what I am. The confusion from my whole day seems to be surrounding everything I do.

My heart's pounding, and I hate that Tobin saw Weston here, but I shouldn't. That's why I was so horrible at the end of us. We went from not knowing how to talk, to me unleashing every fear, hurt and frustration I had. My heart broke as I did it. I knew everything would be easier if Tobin hated me…until I saw him again. I wish I still wanted him to hate me now, because if he didn't before, the hard look on his face when I got out, solidified that how I'd hurt him was all still there.

What Tobin doesn't know is I feel the same way— hurt, angry. I've just learned to be a lot better at pretending.

We probably would have survived my family's move. I know he loved me. I know he would've waited for me until we came back from D.C., but there was a lot more to overcome than miles. And that's the part he bailed on.

Weston and Dad are pulling suitcases out of the

trunk of his car, and I'm standing in the roadway, watching each piece of luggage hit the driveway, wondering how long exactly they plan on staying here.

Weston with his neatly trimmed brown hair, and perfectly shaved face, and tidy clothes—even Tobin all dressed up has something rough around the edges. And it may have been the bit of slouch that attracted me to Weston, but that wouldn't be noticed by anyone in Crawford. Weston here is all polish and rich perfection.

As Dad and Weston joke about something in the driveway, all I can think about is what it was like to say goodbye to Tobin. It happened where they're standing.

Dad sat in the driver's seat waiting. It was one of those horrible early hours of the morning that no one should be awake.

Tobin's grasp on my hip tightened and he pulled me in close as he whispered, "Don't worry, Delia. I'll make this okay."

I believed him. Tobin always made things okay, he'd just been busy, distant. We weren't over, we'd just been under a lot of pressure. I knew as I thought those things that they were excuses. He was wimping out. Leaving me. But the longer he held me, almost desperate, the more I wanted to believe that we were still okay.

I imagined feeling those strong arms wrapped around me almost daily when we first got to D.C. Wishing

Tobin was there to hold me up. Wishing we could just go back to before things got so out of control, when we felt like things were still fixable.

But it was the thing he wouldn't talk about. The thing that I can't bring myself to think about. That's what kept us from trying after I moved. Maybe me leaving town was a relief for both of us.

Neither Tobin nor I knew how to deal with something so much bigger than us, but I'd wanted him to know. I'd wanted him to take care of me, to tell me what to do, and he didn't. I was dealing with too much, and the move to D.C., the move away from home, and I needed him. The harder I held him, the more I more I could feel myself breaking. His lips pressed to mine, and he backed away.

"Bye, Delia," he whispered, and let Mom lead me to the car.

I knew I wasn't good enough for Tobin—he was letting me go.

I'm actually still amazed Dad let him come say goodbye, but I paid for that one later, too.

The shocking realization hit me as I climbed in the car. Tobin hadn't known what to do with our situation, and he hadn't known what to do with me.

The hurt dug in further. It was the first time I thought that Tobin and I might not be able to survive our situation. My body shook in its first sob.

It was like once I left, with all that weight hanging between us—everything I went through without him—we forgot how to talk to each other, and then he called.

Tobin didn't know Weston and I weren't dating when that photo was taken, but my silence to him was a confirmation of what he'd called to find out. And that sealed it.

Tobin had every reason in the world to hate me.

- - -

"Hi Delia!" Weston smiles wide. "Surprise."

"Hey." Weston doesn't belong in Crawford, but I stumble toward him anyway.

He wraps me up in his arms as soon as I'm close enough. "I'm sorry about your friend. I wasn't thinking you were as close as you were," he whispers. "I can't be here the whole time you're here, but I want to help, Delia. I was on my way when we spoke earlier. I'll have to take off probably Saturday or Sunday, meet my dad in Baton Rouge, and then up to Tennessee, and down to Atlanta, but I'm here for now."

Tears start sliding down my cheeks, but I don't think it has anything to do with Eamon, Weston, or Tobin. It has everything to do with confusion.

Weston and I sit on the front porch holding hands while Mom and Dad argue inside. He's politely ignoring the loud voices like I knew he would, but I can't. Neither of us speaks. I start laughing because it's such an absurd situation. We're being so polite in front of the house, while the inside is a mess. It's a metaphor for so many different things that I don't even know where to start.

"You okay, Delia?" Weston's hand squeezes mine. I let myself really look into his dark brown eyes as he rubs his thumb over the back of my hand. My laughter fades slowly.

"You're not tryin' to ignore that, are you?" I tilted my head back to the house.

A soft smile slowly spreads. "Your accent. It's cute. It's been a while since I've heard you talk like that."

Heat slides up my cheeks.

"Don't be embarrassed." He kisses my cheek. "It reminds me of when we first met."

"Right." I nod. "The *informal* barbeque."

He chuckles and lets go of my hand to put his arm around me. I snuggle into the warmth of someone safe because Weston's been my refuge for a long time.

The invitation said informal barbeque at Senator Willis' home in Virginia. Dad was thrilled to be invited to his house, as was Mom. They both dressed for a late dinner at the country club, but I didn't see the point when the invitation said informal. I'd left my cut-offs at home in

Louisiana, but still wore shorts and a simple button-up shirt. I thought I was adding something nice with my chunky wedge sandals.

Dad frowned.

Mom said I was pretty enough that no one would care.

Well, when we got there, I cared. The lawn felt like a golf course it was so massive, littered with perfect white tents, waiters with flutes of champagne and hors d'oeuvres.

The girls my age were all in dressed like I'd never seen. In fabric so soft that I'd be afraid to touch it, much less wear it. No comfy sandals for them either. Their shoes had higher heels than their mothers' did. I wanted to hide in the car.

Mom and Dad stood under the tent talking to people that Dad watched on the news channels. I was still in disbelief that this was supposed to be my new life. I watched the people who looked about my age—all miniature versions of their parents. I'd never felt more out of place, or more like the small town girl that I suddenly knew I was. Standing next to Dad while he gave a small speech in Crawford made me feel important. Special. At that barbeque, I'd felt lower than low.

"Don't worry," a boy whispered behind me, "you're still the prettiest girl here."

I turned and met Weston for the first time. His cheeks were pink, and I guessed that was pretty forward for him. He had short, dark hair, a fairly average build, and deep, brown eyes.

"You're Delia Gentry, am I right?" he asked.

"Yeah..." I took a deep breath and tried to push away my southern drawl, because that's what it suddenly felt like. A drawl. "Yes. I am."

"Our fathers work together. We might end up being friends." He smiled and stuck his hand out for me to shake. "I'm Weston."

I pulled a deep breath in and let myself relax for probably the first time since our move, and shook his hand.

"Hint for you." He stood next to me and rested his hands in his pockets. It was the first time I noticed that he was the most casually dressed of the guys there—his shirt might have been plucked from the floor, and his khakis were in need of a wash. The familiarity felt good.

"Hint for me?" I prompted, as his brown eyes didn't leave mine.

"Oh. Right." He shook his head and smiled. "When you're not sure about something, just raise your chin a bit, and always look them in the eye. I have a feeling you could pull a bluff on any girl here."

And that, at least, was something I could understand.

- - -

"Wanna come upstairs?" I ask Weston, still leaning

into his warmth.

"What, *now*?" His brows come up.

"Scared?" I tease as I stand. My dress is wrinkled, and I'm not sure why I haven't bothered to change.

"No. I just worry about what your parents will think." He follows me through the front door. "Your dad walked me to my room and very specifically said that's where I was staying."

Mom and Dad's voices echo in from the living room—still angry. I'm guessing that Mom came home and drank more than she needed to maintain. I think normally her haze helps her deal with Dad, but when she drinks too much, they argue because she doesn't stay quiet. Dad doesn't like it when Mom's not quiet. Sometimes I hate him.

"I think my parents are busy." I try to make light. "And when they're done fighting, there's usually some time where they're making up. They won't notice." I bite my lip and head toward the stairs. "Besides, you're two years older, and my dad practically worships your father. I think we're okay."

He sighs. "I'm coming."

Weston and I have been dating for almost a year. Since not long after the barbeque, and partly because our parents worked so closely together. We were just together a lot. But it took Weston a long time to hold my hand, and even longer to kiss me.

I cried all night after our first kiss, feeling guilty. And then my guilt made me angry. There was no reason I shouldn't kiss whomever I wanted. Tobin had hung up on me angry more than a month before.

Weston follows me into my room, and I close the door.

I just need some distraction. I need for Weston to light up those butterflies inside me, or to make me forget where I am. When I turn around he looks wary.

"I shouldn't be in here, Delia."

Always the gentleman. This is what girls are supposed to like. We're supposed to swoon over the boys who are always trying to do the right thing. And for the right reasons, even. Instead I kiss him. The next kiss, I kiss him deeper and pull him onto the bed.

Weston and I have never gone all the way. Part of me wonders if guilt will rip me from the inside like it did after our first kiss.

The thing with Weston is that once he lets loose a bit, it feels like he sort of forgets me. And in minutes of being on my bed, that's where we're at. His mouth is hard on mine, and his hands feel desperate against me. I stare at the ceiling as his mouth trails down my neck and across my exposed collarbone.

I'm still not feeling it. Maybe if I close my eyes. Relax into him more. But I close my eyes and Tobin's there. *Of course he is*. Being with Tobin was never something

I could or would have been detached from. He'd kiss my mouth so softly, and then instead of devouring me, it's like he wanted to touch his lips everywhere. To savor each moment of being close.

⌒⌒

Tobin traced my palms running butterflies up my arms, stealing my breath. His lips touched me next—sliding along the trail his fingers did. He always breathed in at my wrists, to take in whatever scent I wore. His hands squeezed mine as he laced our fingers together, and his lips touched the soft skin in the crook of my elbow, working their way up my bicep, across my collarbone and then up my neck.

Tobin always took his time until I forced him to do otherwise.

"A woman is a beautiful thing, Delia. I just wanna appreciate you a little bit." The corner of his mouth pulled up in a half-smirk.

"How many times have you used that line?" I laughed. I knew Tobin wasn't exactly new at this.

His eyes locked with mine.

"Be serious, Delia. You're not like anyone else. Never have been."

"Fine, just don't be such a tease," I joked.

He teased me, or *appreciated* me—kissing up my neck, and I parted my lips, waiting to taste him again, but he moved way. Soft kisses trailed across my chest, between my breasts and down my stomach. His fingers traced invisible lines everywhere—under my belly button and down the outer edges of my thighs, the inner sides of my thighs… Each second counted for something. Every single time.

- - -

"You still with me, Delia?" Weston's pulled away, but our bodies still touch as he leans down and kisses me softly.

"What?" I ask.

He grins wider. "That look on your face—like you were in a different place." He leans up on an elbow. "That's how you make me feel, Delia. I love you."

I smile up at him, not because I feel my smile, but because I know I should. Have I always felt this half-nothing toward him?

"Delia?" He runs a hand through my hair.

"Yeah. I love you, too. Just tired." I sigh and let my body sink deeper into my mattress. What's wrong with me? I was the one who invited him in here.

"I wish I could stay, but—"

"But probably best that you take your own room. We wouldn't want to ruin appearances." Also, I want to be alone.

He scowls. "What's going on? Is that what this

place does to you?"

Weston could be my father in this second, and I open my mouth to scream that this is where I grew up, and he should show some respect, but I know better. Its all part of pretending everything is perfect—something I've learned from Mom. "Just tired." I'm pathetic.

"All right. I'll leave you. I wouldn't want you to be dealing with puffy eyes in the morning." His thumbs brush across my cheeks.

I open my mouth again to tell him that I'm here for a funeral, and it's perfectly acceptable for me to have puffy eyes but don't. Why am I so bitter, and how did everything get so mixed up?

"Goodnight. Thank you." But I just want him to go. To let me be alone.

His fingers brush up and down my arm a few times, and he slides his hand through my hair as I close my eyes. "You're so beautiful," he whispers.

Now I want to cry. He's not a bad guy, and probably if I had the guts to tell him what I wanted, he'd do it. Or he'd try. But instead I lie silent and mumble another thank you as he leaves my room.

I roll on my back when he leaves, stare at the ceiling, and know I need out.

THE MESS

Tugs at my heart
Pulls at my wings
Tells me to run
Tells me to hide
Breaking of souls
Destroyer of love
Unspoken words
Untold lies
The harder the hurt
The harder the fall
The strength to stand up
But no longer fly

I think this proves that I'm completely wrecked.

9

Tobin

I pull up to my house and park next to Eamon's black Jeep. I'd gone to Traive's house to pick it up yesterday before the visitation. I wonder what my parents are planning to do with it—if they've even noticed that it's back. I pause at the front door, unsure of what I'll be walking in to. It's late; my parent's would normally be long asleep by this hour. But can you really sleep the night before your oldest son's funeral?

The mail is piling up on the small table in the entryway. I'll have to go through it in the next day or two before something is turned off for not getting paid. I hang my keys on the hook next to Eamon's and pause outside the kitchen, listening to my parents' hushed voices.

"I just don't understand how this happened," my mom says, her words weighted with drowsiness.

She isn't going to understand. Ever. I don't know why she's even trying to. Nothing that happened that night will ever make sense. Not to her and not to me. I know he was crazy as hell, but playing chicken on the railroad tracks?

Leslie said he had his back turned. It didn't seem like he heard the train. How is that possible? And if he *did* hear it, why didn't he move? He had nothing to prove to anyone. We all got it. You're a badass. How the fuck could you not hear it? How could you not feel the tracks vibrating beneath your feet? How could you think it was worth it to stand firmly there—until you weren't?

∽

I was on my way home from work when I saw Leslie on the side of the road. There was an ambulance and a cop car parked a little ways up. It took me a minute to process what I was seeing, so I had to slam on my brakes and pull off to the side and run back toward her. She was on her hands and knees, dry heaving onto the asphalt in between wails of agony.

"Tobin?" Leslie said when she saw me walking toward her. "Tobin, they told me to wait up here. You shouldn't go down there."

I stared down into the ditch, looking for whoever 'they' were, but the trees and grasses were too thick there. I couldn't see anything but light behind the woods.

"Leslie, what's going on?" Her long hair was stringy and damp with tears. She either didn't hear me, or she didn't know how to respond. "Leslie, where's Traive?" Traive and Leslie had gotten married while they were still in high school. I don't think I'd ever seen one without the other. She gulped loudly.

"The train..." gulp, wail, cough, "he didn't move

when the...the..." She crouched back down and I realized I wasn't going to get anywhere with her. I pulled off my hoodie and wrapped it around her shoulders. I wasn't sure if she was shaking because she was cold or not, but I had to do something before I left her sitting there.

I jogged down the hill and through the trees. The branches whipped across my arms and the bushes scratched at my legs. When I got to a clearing, I was blinded by the spotlight from the train stopped on the tracks. I had to step over piles of beer bottles that littered the ground. There was a cop talking to the driver of the train. I could tell by his uniform that he worked for the railroad. His hand was on his shiny forehead and he just kept shaking it back and forth. It was then that it finally dawned on me. It hadn't been more than two hours since I'd last talked to Eamon.

"Wanna get a beer after I get off of work?" I'd asked.

"Nah, man. I'm meeting up with Traive and Leslie. We're gonna have a few drinks, maybe go sleep out at their camp. You game?"

I passed. I had to work in the morning. So where was Traive now? What the hell happened here? I made my way toward the cop.

Crunch. Crunch. Crunch. The gravel near the tracks crunched under my heavy boots and alerted him that I was coming. He looked up.

"Son, you can't be down here," he said.

"I'm just looking for my friend. What's going on?" I kept my eyes fixed on the train. Even though it was parked and obviously not going anywhere, it's size made me nervous.

The train track arms regularly malfunctioned up on the main road, staying down with lights flashing for days sometimes. Everyone else would pause before weaving around them and continuing on their way. I couldn't. I came to a complete stop and waited. And waited. Until someone honked, annoyed by my caution.

"Tobin?" Traive's voice came out of the darkness to my left. He half-ran, half-stumbled toward me.

"Are you okay, dude? Your wife is up there hyperventilating," I said to him with a small chuckle.

The closer he got, the more I could tell that things were definitely not okay. His eyes were red and wild.

"Tobin," he repeated. He latched on to me, and I couldn't help but feel a little awkward by the show of affection. My eyes searched the woods as he sobbed into my shoulder.

And then I saw it.

A single Chuck Taylor. Faded. Blue. Tossed to the side of the tracks. With no owner.

"Wait," I pushed away from Traive. "Wait!" I

repeated. My brain was trying to process everything, but at the same time trying to deny what I thought I knew.

"Where's Eamon?" I yelled.

"We tried to tell him, Tobin. We yelled. I tried to go to him, but Leslie wouldn't let me. He just didn't move," Traive said.

I felt the woods start to spin. I really took in the scene. The medics on the other side of the train. The stretcher. It was covered with a sheet.

There was something under it.

Someone.

My brother.

- - -

"Tobin, you home, baby?" Mom calls.

I take one more deep breath and round the corner into the kitchen. Mom and Dad are sitting at the breakfast table with plates of untouched food in front of them. The trashcan is overflowing. The only light on is the one above the sink. Its bulb is about to burn out so it flashes every few seconds, making the entire scene even that much more pitiful.

"Hey Mama," I say. I stand behind her and start to rub her shoulders, but she feels too frail. I stop, afraid I'll hurt her.

"Are you hungry?" she asks.

"No, Ma'am. I ate earlier," I say.

Dad is silently staring down at his plate. I want to tell him that he needs to snap out of it. That he needs to be strong for Mom. But who am I to say that? I don't know what I'd do if I were in his shoes. I'm having a hard enough time keeping it together. How can I expect my dad to?

I push the trash down into the can and tie up the bag before putting a fresh one in. I glance into the sink, but there are no dirty dishes. No one is eating in this house. I sort of don't know what to do. Several minutes pass and the ticking clock above the stove is the only noise in the room.

"It sure was nice to see Delia and her mama tonight. It was so sweet of them to make the trip," Mom says.

I long for the painful silence of just seconds ago.

"Yep," is all I have to offer.

"Do you think she'll be at the service in the morning?" Mom asks.

I hadn't thought that far ahead. I didn't have a chance to ask her before I left her earlier. Jesus, what if she shows up with her boyfriend? Nah, she wouldn't do that. She's got more class than to show up to a funeral with a date like it's some society function.

"No idea," I say.

"Did y'all talk about... How is she feeling?" Mom can't bring herself to say the words. She never has been able to.

"She's good."

"Do you need me to press a shirt for you for tomorrow?" Mom asks.

"No, Mama. I've got it under control."

She nods. I should have said yes. The woman has no purpose right now. She yawns deeply and then lays her head down on the table top.

"Tobin, I'd like you to say a few words about your brother tomorrow. It'd mean a lot to me," Mom says. The thought of standing in front of a church full of people, talking about my dead brother makes me feel nauseous.

"Ma, isn't there someone else? Traive? Uncle James?" Someone. *Anyone* other than me?

"He was your brother," she says, like this is something that had never dawned on me before now. The use of past tense is a new thing, though.

Was. Will I ever get used to it?

"Yes, Ma'am," I say.

She makes an expression like she's trying to smile, but it just won't work, so it comes off looking more like a grimace.

"Can I help you to bed?" She's got to be able to sleep. The purple circles under her eyes are so deep they look painful.

"I'll do it," Dad finally speaks. He pulls Mom's chair out and helps her stand. He pats me on the shoulder before they hobble out of the kitchen and up the stairs, holding on to each other. Keeping each other moving forward. Keeping each other alive. I don't know what that's like. The last time I felt like I had someone depend on me like that, she up and bailed, quickly finding someone new to take care of her. I guess it wasn't what I thought it was.

I contemplate what to do next. I know if I go upstairs, I'm going to have to listen to my mom cry herself to sleep like she's done the last several nights. I don't have anywhere to go and don't really want to be around anyone, but I can't stay here.

I grab my wallet out of the dish by the door and the keys to my truck and slip out into the dark.

THE FALL

The fall of a lifetime
The fall of a girl
The fall from her window
For a different world

The touch of a boy
Like she'd never had
But the way he left her
~~Made her sad~~
~~Was really bad~~

I suck. This is crap.
You said they wouldn't all be good, and that it was okay.
I'm just not sure if I still believe you.

10

Delia

I miss the way Tobin smelled when he'd come home from work. Like metal, sweat, and fire. I loved what his welding job did to his arms, shoulders, and back. Kelly, Rachel, and I would walk in front of the welding shop a hundred times a day just to smile, or wave. That was the summer Tobin and I got together. The summer that forever changed my life. The last year I spent in Crawford. And I spent as much of it with Tobin as I could.

My favorite time to watch him work was when Tobin couldn't see me, and I was alone. I'd just watch for a few moments. Even with his mask on, I could tell he was deep into his work. He was an artist as much as he was a builder or repairer. Something I don't think most people recognized about him. I know my dad didn't.

I thought once we got back to town, it would seem more real, but even being here, it still seems impossible that Eamon's gone. I hate that he's gone. I hate it for young men everywhere, and for me and for Tobin and for the people who Eamon helped find strength, even when they didn't think they had any.

Tobin did that for me. I was never stronger, happier, and more alive than when I was with those two—

even though I don't think Eamon had any idea what to do with the way

Tobin and I felt about each other.

Eamon took me in like one of his own, because even though he thought we were crazy, he could see how much I loved his brother.

Tobin was the only thing I ever stood up to my dad for. Even if I only did a crap job of it, I tried. Until suddenly Dad seemed right, and I was just too tired to fight anymore.

ᐉᵕᑐ

"The only time we've been at odds, Delia, was over that boy." Dad stood in the doorway of my new room in D.C. as I laid in bed, my whole body aching. It wasn't just the move, all of it was too much for me to deal with.

I wiped more tears, but didn't say anything.

"I want you to think about how that turned out, Delia. Think about it long and hard. I want you to know that taking over Senator Lyle's seat was an honor I was chosen for, and I'm not going to be one of those men making excuses for my kids because I expect you'll damn well do what I tell you to." Dad's jaw was set, his dark hair greased back, and his three-hundred dollar custom shirt was pressed and heavily starched to perfection.

I wanted to scream at him and tell him I hated him and that I'd do whatever I damned well pleased, but Tobin wasn't there. Tobin hadn't called.

Tobin broke my heart before I broke his, he just didn't see it that way. He said he couldn't answer when I'd called, that he needed space, time to process what was going on with us. But I needed him. For him to finally decide to be there after I was gone was too little too late. I figured he would be relieved. He was finally rid of me.

"We understand each other, Delia?" I swear Dad grew a foot taller as he leaned into my room.

"Yes sir." I wanted to snap out the words, but instead I sounded weak. Just like he wanted me to. Damn Tobin. I'd needed him to fight, and he'd just let me go. He had to know that I couldn't be strong anymore. That I didn't know how to stand up to my dad without him by my side.

Mom stepped through the door, not meeting's Dad's glare. She patted him on the arm. "I'll talk to her."

"Delia and I have already talked!" His voice boomed. "And she knows damn well what I expect. We have a dinner tomorrow night, and she needs to be cleaned up and ready to go."

I wondered if by 'clean up' Dad meant that he'd noticed that I was wearing one of Tobin's shirts. I stole it from his room the day before we left town. It was the only thing I'd ever taken without permission from anyone. The soft, button up plaid shirt was old and worn and smelled deliciously like Tobin.

Most of the time, I kept it folded in the back of my

closet, not wanting to wear it too much and have the smell of him wear away. But on really bad days, I couldn't help but put it on. Wanting any shred of him to be there with me.

Dad disappeared, and I broke down into a fit of sobs that tugged and pulled at my insides. Who still thought this way—that their family was there to serve them or something? Everything about being in D.C. felt backwards.

Mom was quiet, as always, but rested a hand on my shoulder. "You have to understand Delia. Your father was raised by a very harsh man and has worked really hard to get to where he is."

At that moment I hated Tobin for backing away almost as much as I hated Dad for pushing me forward. I wanted to scream at Mom that I didn't care about Dad and where he was from. He should already see that he'd taken everything from me.

And as Mom sat next to my bed trying to explain away her husband's behavior, she pulled another long drink from the cup she'd left on my nightstand.

All I knew in that moment was that I was too tired to fight anymore. I'd fought for time with Tobin. I'd fought for Tobin. I'd fought for control of this situation that we put ourselves in. But Dad was right—*where was Tobin now, when I needed him?*

- - -

I roll over in bed and try to get comfortable again, but I can't do it.

Out. Out. Out. It's all I can think as I slide off my mattress.

This routine I could do in my sleep. I lock my door, go the bathroom and smear a few drops of jasmine oil on my wrists before I remember I'm not meeting anyone and don't need to do that.

I glance around at the pink. Tobin gave me so much crap over my pink bedroom and bathroom. I used to tell him over and over that I picked it all out when I was fourteen and couldn't be held liable. I think he used it as an excuse to tease me.

Weston hadn't said a thing. He'd never been to this house, and never said a thing about my ridiculously girly room. Damn, Tobin for still being in my head.

I still don't know if Tobin's just a part of this place, or more a part of me than I realized. Either way, his name brings equal amounts of pain and something I don't understand.

My soft cut-offs are where I left them in my closet, and they're a little big from my salad and coffee diet, but they'll stay on. In minutes I'm sitting on the edge of my window, waiting for the courage to drop down. I've done this a million times. A *million.*

But I can't do it. It's too far. *Tobin's not waiting to catch me.*

I'm pissed at myself when I slide back inside. Now what am I going to do?

The obvious answer hits me.

Go out the front door.

The house is silent as I sneak through, until my hand hits the front door, and someone clears their throat. My stomach seizes up at the thought of being caught. Dad was one thing, Weston would probably be another. He'd want to come, or keep me inside, and I can't stand the thought of either.

I spin around and see Mom in her bathrobe, leaning against the counter with a mug in her hands watching me. She's drinking in the middle of the night. I think this is new, but not positive.

"I…" I start to whisper.

She shakes her head, a tiny smile on the edge of her mouth. "Be quiet when you come back. I'll leave the door unlocked." Her voice isn't even a whisper, and I wonder if I heard her right.

My jaw drops. I'm a bit shocked, and bewildered, but I'll take it. I think I nod or wave or react in some way before tiptoeing out the door, and closing it silently behind me. It makes me wonder what it would have been like if Mom had been the one who caught me sneaking back in that first time, instead of Dad.

✺

The first time I got caught sneaking out was awful. Well, I was actually trying to sneak back in. I saw my dad on the porch before Tobin did. He always walked me back home—unless he was too drunk, in which case I'd leave him with Eamon, making him promise me he wouldn't try some dumb stunt while taking Tobin back to his bed. That had only happened a couple of times. The morning I got caught, Tobin was with me.

I stopped in the woods, in the faintest beginnings of dawn, and Dad's anger radiated from that porch like nothing I'd ever felt.

"Oh, Shit. Delia, I'm sorry. I'll come up with you." His hand squeezed mine and the other touched the ends of my hair.

I'd almost laughed. If I hadn't been so scared, I would have. "I don't think that'll help."

Dad hadn't seen me yet, probably wasn't sure which direction he should be looking. I hated our vast lawn right then. If the trees were closer to the house, I might have had a chance to sneak onto the back porch and claim to have slept there all night.

"A kiss then, and call me when you can." Tobin's fingers slid around the top of my jeans sending a shiver through my body.

I turned to kiss him, and as usual, he was already waiting for it. He could never get enough of me, he'd always said.

—

92

Just another reason that I felt invincible with Tobin. Dad's voice split the silence just as our lips came together.

"DELIA GENTRY, YOU GET UP TO THIS HOUSE RIGHT NOW!"

I jumped out of Tobin's arms and started running without a glance back. Dad was not to be messed with.

My heart pounded so hard that I could hear the *thump-thump* pulsating in my ears, I had no idea what I'd say to him. He'd really caught me in the worst possible way.

"Not you!" Dad yelled again. "Get out of here, and go home!"

I turned to see Tobin following me.

"Please go," I whispered, desperately afraid for what Dad would do to him.

"I'm not letting you take the fall for this, Delia."

I was so torn then. The love in Tobin's eyes versus the anger in my dad's.

Dad was between us before I knew he'd moved, grabbing us each by arm, pushing Tobin away and pulling me behind him in one quick, fluid movement.

"I'm only going to tell you this once, son." I could barely see Tobin behind my dad's large frame. "You keep your hands off my daughter. You're a piece of shit in a small town, and no part of you is worthy of her. Got it?"

Even Tobin didn't have anything to say to that.

My heart broke at both my dad's words and the expression on Tobin's face.

I opened my mouth and tried to speak, tried to defend him, but Dad was too scary. Still is.

Dad grabbed my arm and led me inside. I stared at Tobin the whole way, just praying he wouldn't let me go. Wouldn't let my dad stand between us.

He didn't.

Dad was gone enough that we still managed to find time. But I sometimes wonder what my dad's words did to him. Or if they ever talked when I wasn't around. Tobin never mentioned it, and neither did I.

- - -

I actually have to wipe away tears from the memory. Tobin deserved better than that from Dad, and I should have said something. Done something. Fought harder for Tobin.

The trail he and I used is still here, but overgrown, which makes me sad. Not that I could have expected anything different. There isn't another head-over-heels-in-love girl staying in my room in need of this trail right now.

The night is so much quieter here than in D.C. Dad wanted to be downtown—where the action is. Our place is huge and has an incredible view of the National Monument. I love and hate that home. Love it because everyone loves it, and probably I hate it for the same reason.

When I hit the railroad tracks, my stomach tightens. Eamon died along here somewhere. Maybe I don't want to be here. Once I get to the bridge over the creek I follow it toward the lake. I can lose myself there for a while instead. I just have to make sure I'm back before everyone's awake.

I know I might just be torturing myself, but all I can think about is getting to our favorite spots. Seeing them again – the things I miss most about Crawford. Maybe I need a quick trip to the bar first. It's been ages since I had a beer.

"If it isn't the great Delia Gentry, come back to slum it up." Carl, the bar owner, laughs as I walk in. "Are you old enough to be in here?" he teases.

"You didn't have a problem with it a year ago." I raise a brow and take a seat at the bar. I love this old place. Its run down, and always smells like cigarette smoke, but I used to pass through here a lot.

"That was more than a year." Carl turns away, dries a glass, and sets it back on the shelf. The tone of his voice tells me he might be a bit irritated. Or maybe it's that his loyalties to Tobin run deep. Everyone knows that we're not together anymore. In this small of a town, there are no secrets. Except maybe one. One that my dad, the staunch Pro-Life Republican would do anything to keep from coming to light.

I start to wonder if underneath the surface everyone here suddenly hates me.

"Did you drive here, Delia?" Carl asks as he fills a glass of beer and hands it to one of the three other people at the bar.

"No." I almost laugh. "Not with my jail-keeper." And then my hand flies to my mouth because I've gotten so good at never saying anything bad about Dad.

He chuckles. "Did you or did you not graduate, Miss Delia?" He rests his elbows on the bar, smiling with stained teeth, his blondish-grey hair so short I see more scalp than hair.

"I did." But it doesn't matter. Not to Dad. "But with his job—"

Carl shakes his head. He sees how much of a wimp I am. Not hard if you're looking.

"Any chance of getting a beer from you?" I do my best smile and lean over the counter, wondering if a little bit of cleavage will help. I feel completely, scandalously, naughty, and so much of me wishes I was still this girl. Could still *be* this girl.

If Weston saw me now... He doesn't even know this Delia exists.

Carl gives me a smile and walks away.

So much for my beer.

"Delia!"

I spin and squint to see Nelson, a good friend of both Tobin and Eamon, waving.

"I want to feel like a man. Come over here and let me kick your ass at bowling, would ya?" He slaps the side of a table against the wall.

I stand up and move toward him. "Bowling?"

He rolls his eyes, and lets his head follow. "Shuffleboard bowling? Damn. How long you been gone?"

"Too long." I laugh.

"Delia?" Carl holds up an ice-cold Corona.

"Thanks!" I grin and jog up to the bar, immediately popping the top. Carl always said if he didn't open it, he could always say we just stole it.

"So, you game?" Nelson asks.

I glance back toward the door. Back to Carl standing behind the dark, wooden bar.

"Got somewhere to be?" he asks.

I want to laugh and giggle and jump. "No. *Nowhere* to be."

"Well, let's get started then." Everywhere Tobin's southern accent is soft, Nelson's twangs, but it's such a part of him that I love it.

"Yeah. Let's play." I step up to the table, take a long drink of my cold beer, and can't believe how long I've stayed away.

11

Tobin

The bar scene in Crawford is limited, but that's okay. I'm not looking to have a good time anyway. I pull a napkin from the stack on the end of the bar and spread it out.

"Tobin! Surprised to see you here. I was real sorry to hear about your brother, man," Carl, the owner and lone employee of the one and only bar in town says. He's frowning at me, his eyes full of pity.

I hate pity.

"Thanks, Carl," I say, and shake his hand.

"Well, what can I get you? It's on the house tonight. Your brother was a good man," he says.

Was he? I wonder. I mean, he was my brother, of course I loved him, but do good men leave their mom's mourning them because they were too stubborn to step away from an oncoming train?

"Just a beer. Whatever you have in a bottle is fine. Oh, and an ink pen," I say.

He pulls a pen from his shirt pocket and pops the cap off of a beer bottle and slides them across the bar to me.

I take a long pull from the bottle. It's not entirely cold, but it doesn't matter.

I stare down at the blank napkin. What can I write about Eamon that can be said in front of a church full of people?

Eamon was always there for people when they needed him.

I write across the flimsy napkin. I stare at what I've written. Lies. I draw a thick line through the words. If Eamon cared about being there for people he would be here now. Sitting next to me. Telling me about his latest conquest. Or arguing about who was going to win the game on Monday. No, those weren't important things in the grand scheme of things, but *I* was. Brothers were supposed to be important. I wad the napkin up and shove it into my jeans pocket.

"Hey bro!" I flinch at the word *bro* like I've just been punched. Nelson Gautreaux has pulled up the stool next to me.

"Hey man, I didn't see you come in," I say. To be fair, I wasn't looking. I was too busy trying to write a eulogy for my real *bro.*

"I've been here all night," he says.

Of course he has. This town doesn't have much else to offer. I should've just gone out to the lake. It was my first thought. It'd be a quiet place to get my thoughts together and write something for the funeral. But I knew she'd be there. Not literally.

I'm sure Delia is back at her house—her parents thinking she's tucked safely into her bed, though she probably snuck in to be with her boyfriend. At least that's something the Delia I knew would do. With me. I shudder. But the *feeling* of her haunts our spot out at the lake.

Most days I'm okay with the lingering sensation that she could walk up any second and I could coax her into going for a swim—for starters. That first night that I met her out on the dock was only the first of many, but it's a night that every detail is burned into my memory.

I'd bet her she wouldn't go in the water, but she surprised me by beating me to it. I always think of the way she looked in the near blackness of the night as she climbed out of the water in nothing more than her flesh colored bra and panties.

Her long, dark hair was wet and stuck to her chest; beads of water ran down her stomach. She was incredibly sexy. I knew she was out of her element that night. Acting brave. But doing it for me. Because if Delia Gentry were the kind of girl to strip down in front of people, I definitely would have heard.

Being with Delia was like always walking a thin

line between innocence and sin. Things that I'd done with a dozen girls before her were suddenly new and sacred. Every touch meant something. Even on that first night.

⌒

I purposely got out of the water before she did so that I could sit on the dock and watch her climb up the ladder. She was unbelievably hot. I can't believe I hadn't hung out with her before. Well, I guess I could believe it. From what Eamon told me, her dad kept a short leash on her and controlled who she spent time with.

That should have deterred me right off the bat, and it might have—if I hadn't already seen her strip down and run into the water. If I hadn't watched the way she threw her head back when she laughed. If I didn't see her blush when I told her that she was the most beautiful thing I'd ever seen. And if I hadn't meant it.

After all of that, I knew I was in it, no matter who her father was.

"Brrr!" she squeaked. "It's freezing!" She clutched her arms across her stomach and jumped up in down in place, beads of water falling from her skin and hair. I wanted to pull her in close to me. Well, if I'm honest, I wanted to do more than that.

She looked around the dock, "Where's my shirt?"

I raised my eyebrow and grinned.

"Your shirt for a kiss," I said.

She laughed, that perfect, genuine laugh. "I'm not sure that's a fair trade."

"Why is that?" I asked. I dangled her shirt up above our heads, much too high for her to reach even if she were to jump.

"Because I was going to give you one anyway," she said through chattering teeth. She smiled that same daring smile she had earlier.

I reached for her, and she shivered, so I wrapped my dry shirt around her. I leaned down and my mouth barely brushed hers before she pulled back. It was the quickest kiss I'd ever had, but it changed me. And her standing right there, staring up at me was pure torture.

Her eyes were smiling and I thought for sure she was screwing with me. Had the whole night had been a joke to her?

"Holy shit," she said.

And I had to agree.

I wrapped my arms around her waist and pulled her in close. My thumbs grazed along her hipbones, and this time, she stood up on her tip-toes to meet my lips with hers.

- - -

"You just missed Delia," Nelson says.

With the mention of her name, my heart hammers in my chest.

"She was here?" I ask.

"Yeah, she schooled me at shuffleboard bowling! I'd been holding that record for the last two years. And that big city girl comes in and whoops my ass! You know what they say, you can take the girl out of the country and all that," he laughs.

Even though it's ridiculous, I feel myself swell with pride that she beat Nelson.

"Where'd she go?" I ask. It doesn't matter; I can't go tracking her down like some lunatic ex-boyfriend, even though that's exactly what I feel like.

"Said she was going home, had to get up early for…you know…" he fumbles over his words and stares down at his boots.

"Right," I say. I finish off my beer and throw a couple of bucks onto the bar. "Well, it was good seeing you, Nelson."

"Hey, we had planned a bonfire out at my camp tomorrow night. Been having it planned for a while now, and just thought it'd be fitting to still do it in honor of Eamon.

Your girl said she'd be there, so I guess I'll see you then," he says.

I should tell him that Delia is most definitely not mine, but I let it go.

FOR GRANDMA

A woman is
soft
hard
the inbetween
the thing that saves
holds
binds
loves without question
teases without hesitation
smiles without worry
and winks with reckless abandon

I miss you.

12

Delia

The railroad tracks were our meeting grounds since I could remember. It was a bit of a walk for both of us, but the stream that went under the tracks also led into the lake, and Tobin and I spent a *lot* of time in that lake together. It's also the fastest way to get to town aside from walking alongside the road. I walked up the gravel mound the tracks rested on and started balance-walking on the rails.

"Your hand in mine." Tobin would tease, and we'd try to walk on the rails holding hands, but I know Eamon died on these tracks, and suddenly my legs feel weak. Eamon may have died along here somewhere, but this is also when I knew I'd lost my grandma.

My grandma, the *democrat.* The woman who fought with Dad for me when Mom didn't, which was often. The woman who loved Tobin like one of her own.

I stumbled on the railroad tracks, knowing it was the fastest way to Tobin, but not being able to see through my tears. Our phone conversation had been short. Just long enough for him to know my dad was gone, my mom was asleep, and my grandma just died. My legs ran out of strength, and I just sat on the tracks and waited.

Gram had been the first person in my family I

brought Tobin to meet. She'd loved him immediately.

"You may be young, Delia, but you hold on to that boy. He has the kind of heart you don't see in a man very often," she'd said seriously.

I'd laughed, but I knew exactly what she meant. I'd felt it too.

"I bet you two will make love with the same passion you fight with." She snickered.

Tobin and I hadn't gone all the way then, and my cheeks flushed hot. "I can't believe you just said that Grandma."

She'd winked and patted my back. That simple memory, pulled me into another round of agony over losing the only person in my family who understood me.

I heard his feet running toward me. Fast. Tobin never hesitated when he knew it was important.

"Delia." His arms came around me where I was crumpled on the ground.

I shook in sobs that I couldn't control. Didn't even *try* to control. My Grandma was my sanity. My safe place. My haven from my parents. She wasn't allowed to die.

He kissed my head and whispered that he'd take care of me. That he wouldn't leave my side until I was okay. His arms held me as tight as I needed them to. Tight enough to keep me together.

We heard the low rumble long before the train came around the bend in the tracks. Tobin stood up, keeping me in his arms. He lifted me like I was nothing and carried me home. No complaints.

He sat with me for two days. He stayed at my house holding me, even though it had to be miserable for him to be there. It was the first time he told me he loved me, and there was no way that I couldn't believe him. Not then. Not in that moment. Not even now.

- - -

It's so much harder being here than I thought it would be.

Instead of continuing to walk, I sit and pull out my phone. I have emails and messages stacked up so high I don't know where to start.

The thing is, now that I'm back home, I don't care about the fundraiser, I never cared about the signatures, and I wonder if I care what they think of me. Mercedes said that in an election year they always lose a few friends. I wondered how you can *lose* a friend, but isn't that exactly what I've done in Crawford?

Kelly, Rachel, and I used to be tight. Really tight. But lately, anything to do with Crawford just hurt too much, and I'd been spending too much time trying to fit in there the way I'd fit in here.

I start typing an automated reply to my email, sort of amazed I even know how to do that.

Delia Gentry is unavailable due to the sudden loss of a close friend. She will begin returning phone calls and emails in...

How long could I get away with? Forever? I laugh.

...two weeks. Thank you, Delia Gentry

I open the text messaging on my phone, pick almost everyone I know from D.C. out of my contacts list, and type in the same thing.

My thumb actually shakes as it hovers over the send button. This is for real. I'm taking two weeks off from being Delia from D.C. The release of weight off my shoulders feels incredible. Amazing. Like I could fly.

I hit send, and shove the phone back in my pocket. It feels good. Such a silly thing for me to stress over—telling people I need time. And not even to their face. But still, I never say no. I dig in and do.

Now that it's done, and I'm free for a while, I take huge juvenile skips a short ways on the tracks just because I'm alone, and I can do whatever I want. My laughter fills the air around me, and I'm in disbelief that I didn't want to come home before now.

The low rumble of a train sends me leaping off the tracks, and another fit of laughter hits me. And then I want to puke as the train flies by. Eamon. Stupid ass. I bet that boy died playing chicken, not whatever BS story that was probably fed to my parents.

There was talk that it was suicide. Never. Eamon would never do that. I don't know what exactly happened out on the tracks, but I know that for certain. He'd never leave his family—his brother, on purpose.

My heart breaks a little for Tobin, but I am so thankful that he wasn't there with his brother that night. There was no limit to what those boys would do for each other, there's no way Tobin would have stood by and watched his brother get hit, he may have very well sacrificed himself trying to save Eamon.

I shudder thinking about losing Tobin, *really* losing him. And just that fast I feel like once again, maybe I shouldn't have come.

"Del-yuh!" Kelly shrieks as her laughter peels through the air. "Come 'ere!!"

"Delia!" Rachel's behind her, and they're holding one another like they need the support to stand up.

I laugh as I head their way. The air is practically flammable from all of the alcohol.

This situation isn't likely to end well.

I trip on the rocks a bit as I jog to where they're half-stumbling over each other.

"Delia." Rachel grabs my shoulders and puts our foreheads together. The smell of cheap whiskey burns my nose, and I try not to laugh. "I was such a bitch at the diner. I mean, seriously. Prom?"

"Rachel." I'm giggling as I put my hands on her shoulders. "It's okay."

"She's had too much to drink," Kelly's shaking in laughter.

"What's going on?" I ask.

"Oh." Rachel sighs before sitting directly in the middle of the tracks, letting her long, skinny legs stretch out in front of her. "It hurts." She punches herself in the chest. "I miss Eamon."

I glance at Kelly hoping for more explanation.

Kelly holds a hand next to her mouth like she's about to tell me a big secret, and we lean toward each other. There's a faint smell of beer on Kelly, but she looks to be pretty sober – at least she's standing upright and leaning toward me without any problem.

"Rachel. You're in rare form tonight." I shake my head, but am also a bit jealous of their freedom.

"Rachel's pretty sure she was the last one who was…uh…*with* Eamon before he died," Kelly tries to explain.

"But you were always such a good girl!" My eyes flash to Rachel, who might be gaining back a tiny bit of her sobriety. She's swaying a little less anyway as she sits on the tracks. I can't believe she'd sleep with Eamon. To say he had a reputation was putting it mildly. You'd get treated like a queen for the night, but he never made any secret that he didn't do relationships. With Eamon, you got what you got. He wasn't an asshole about it either. Just upfront.

"I heard from Leslie that there were just pieces of him left." She makes a sweeping gesture with her hand toward the forest.

Pieces. Yeah. That sounds more like what I thought when I heard the press version of the story. There's a bigger mess behind a lot of what ends up in the paper. Or the paper prints a big mess when there's nothing going on at all.

I feel bad for the girls, but mostly I ache for Tobin.

"Think you could help me get her home?" Kelly asks.

"Yeah. Sure." The smile relaxes through my neck, into my shoulders, and spreads something warm through me.

Happiness, I guess.

Being needed.

Belonging.

"I'll help you get her home."

THERE ONCE WAS A GIRL

There once was a girl with two faces.
Two hearts
Two lives

But the more she lived in the pretend life
The more it became her real one

And the less she thought about her real life
The more it became her pretend one

Her heels towered her to the sky,
and her bare feet anchored her to the ground.

The problem is that she didn't know where she
actually lived – in the clouds, or on the earth

Reality had escaped with the space between the two
girls.

13
Tobin

I guess I should stop drinking. The last thing my parents need is me showing up to Eamon's funeral drunk. I take one last long pull from the bottle and then toss it into the pile along the tracks with the rest of them.

This was our spot, me and D. I check my watch. By now, she's probably snuggled in with the boyfriend. Bet they take off for home tomorrow. The look on that douche bag boyfriend's face told me he didn't show up here to leave empty handed. I run my finger along the smooth velvet of that stupid black box. Almost a smaller version of what my brother is lying in right now. Both containing lifeless, cold things.

My heart strains with the enormous feeling of loss. The box croaks as I open it and stare at that pathetic looking row of diamonds. Every time I look at the ring, I'm forced to remember what I *thought* my future would look like. No more. I've got to forget this girl. I snap it shut once last time and toss it as hard as I can into the darkness. Just how Eamon taught me to throw a baseball when I was a kid. *Keep your elbow above your shoulder. Don't smother the ball. Throw in a low arc, Tobin.*

It's done.

When Delia and I were together, we used take the back road into the woods and I'd park my truck near the tracks. We'd lie in the bed of the truck and watch the trains. Now I'm sitting on the tailgate alone and all I see is Eamon.

The tracks start to vibrate and I close my eyes. The rumble reverberates from one end of the track to the other. How the hell could he not hear it? It's close now. I can feel the vibration within me. The train lets out a loud whistle and the wind kicks up.

My truck shakes as it finally passes and then, just like that, it's quiet again. The only noise is the faint sound of the radio on in the cab of my truck. Zydeco. My lips curl into an involuntary smile. I let myself give into the memory. It's better than sitting here wondering where each part of my brother ended up. With each scrape of the rubboard, I'm closer and closer to that night.

∽

"Come on, Delia," I whispered as loudly as the silent night would allow.

Delia hovered half-in, half-out of her bedroom window. She surveyed the ground for the fiftieth time.

"What if I get caught?" she asked. She bit her bottom lip and checked the ground again.

"You sure as shit will if we spend any more time hanging outside like this. I've got you baby, trust me," I said.

She finally relented and slipped out the window. It wasn't that far of a drop, but for Delia Gentry, who had never broken her daddy's curfew before, it probably felt like leaping off the top of the town water tower.

I caught her, just like I promised her I would.

"You ready?" I asked, clutching her hand.

"I'm a little nervous," she said, tugging on the tips of her bangs.

"Don't be, they'll love you," I assured her. I didn't dare tell her how completely over-dressed she was for a crawfish boil. But she looked freaking gorgeous and I couldn't wait to dance with her.

"Well, no shit!" Eamon yelled from across the old farm. "I thought you were lying when you said you were bringing Miss Priss!"

Delia's eyes widened, and her cheeks went red.

"He means that in the nicest way possible." I leaned in and whispered in her ear. She didn't relax, and her grip on my bicep stayed tight. Eamon was already lit, but was chugging a plastic cup of beer.

"You want a drink, darlin'?" He offered Delia his cup. She gave a sharp, quick shake of her head.

"Come on, I'll get you something," I said, leading her away. Maybe it was a mistake bringing her here.

"Are you hungry?" I asked. I motioned to the piles of crawfish that filled an entire pirot.

Delia whispered something that at first, I didn't hear. And then when I finally realized what she said, I couldn't believe.

"I'm sorry, could you repeat that?" I asked incredulously.

"I said, I've actually never had crawfish." Her eyes darted to each end of the room and back.

It was like something in a movie where the city guy comes into the bar and the music stops. Half the place stopped dancing and turned around to stare. If she wasn't embarrassed before, she sure as shit was now. I felt terrible.

Of course Eamon reappeared.

"Sweetheart, how have you lived in this fine State your entire life, and you have never had crawfish?" Eamon shook his head. "And your daddy claims to represent us."

She bit her lip. "I don't know, I guess I just didn't know how to eat it."

Eamon wrapped his arm around her and led her to a table. He scooped three massive mounds of crawfish onto the red plastic tablecloth and nodded at Delia to sit down. She looked at me in a way that screamed, "do something," but in this case, I couldn't. There was no way I was going to let her go that night without at least trying it.

"All right, so here's what you wanna do." Eamon picked up a large red shell, and Delia reluctantly followed suit. "You gotta hold it on both sides of the tail, twist and snap. Now with your thumbs, peel that shell away from the widest part of the tail just like a shrimp."

"I've never eaten shrimp," Delia said.

Eamon dropped the crawfish and stared at me. "You're killing me, both of you," he said.

"Come on, Eamon, move it along," I said.

"All right, holding the tail, pull out the meat." He popped the tiny morsel into his mouth and moved on to the next shell.

Delia wasn't so impressed. She held the minuscule piece of meat in between her fingers.

"That's it?" she asked with a smile. "All that work for this?"

I laughed. Eamon shook his head.

"You know what the problem is? You need beer," Eamon said.

That was the first night she met everyone. Traive, Leslie, Nelson, all of them took pride in introducing her to something new, knowing that she was special and wasn't going anywhere any time soon.

Eamon walked away and Delia stood to follow him.

I caught her arm just as she passed me and leaned in, my nose buried in her thick hair.

"Get your sexy ass over here and dance with me." I growled into her ear.

I don't think I've ever danced so much in my life as I did that night. I'd barely had anything to drink, but I was drunk off the feeling of Delia close to me and the smell of the jasmine oil that she dabbed on her neck and wrists—

- - -

Jasmine oil.

I swear to God I can smell it in the air right now.

I hop down off of the tailgate and start walking. Now that I'm standing upright, I realize just how much I've had to drink. I glance over my shoulder at the pile of empty bottles. Shit. This close to the tracks, I have a hard time keeping Eamon away. Was this what happened? Was he totally shit faced? No, Traive said he'd only had a beer or two.

I'm stumbling, and for once, I feel scared. I don't want to be here anymore, but there's no way I'm sober enough to drive home. The weight of the grief finally forces me down. I finally give in and let it. I sit down alongside the same damn tracks that my brother died on and sob like a baby.

This wasn't supposed to happen. He was supposed to be here till the end.

And there it is again, that damn smell. I can't get either one of them out of my head. I lost Eamon and now I feel like I'm having to lose Delia all over again. I know what he'd tell me to do. Go out and find a new piece of ass and get the fuck over it. I wish it were that simple.

"Tobin?" Her voice is tiny but shoots through me like an electric shock. I pause before looking up from the gravel. Surely that was the beer talking. She isn't *actually* here.

But when I look up, she *is* standing there. It's not my imagination.

"Delia, go away," I say flatly.

"Tobin, what are you doing? You shouldn't be out here," she says. Her voice is full of pity and it's the last thing in the world that I want from her right now.

I feel her hand on my shoulder and I jerk away.

"Come on, Tobin. Let me take you home," she says.

I can't do a whole lot of arguing. It's already early morning, and I've got to give my brother's eulogy in just a few short hours. I run my forearm across my face to wipe away any tears that may be there. I hope I do it quickly enough that she doesn't notice. What the fuck do I care anyway right now, though?

She wraps her arm around me to help me up.

∽

"Tobin, she was everything to me," she said.

I wiped the tear from under her hazel eye with my thumb and then stroked her chestnut hair. I wanted to tell her that at least her grandmother was away from Delia's asshole of a father now, but refrained. He gave her grandma hell for not rolling over and agreeing with him and what he believed. She was a feisty little woman. I know Delia really looked up to her.

"I know, baby, it's going to be okay, I'm not going to leave you," I told her.

I cradled her in my arms and picked her up off of the ground.

Her grandmother died that summer and there was nothing that I could do to make her feel any better. But I stayed by her side for days despite her father's objections about me being in their house—he was far too busy and important to make the trip back home. He's such a stereotypical, political ass.

I helped her into bed the night before her grandmother's funeral. I fluffed the pillows like I'd seen my mom do when we were having company and pulled the thick down comforter up over her. It was the first time that I'd actually taken care of someone. The first time that someone needed me.

"I love you, Delia Gentry," I told her. My heart raced, I'd never said the words to a woman before.

"So, what, your love for mine? Another trade?" she asked. It was her first smile in days.

"Nope, I love you. That's it." I said.

"Well, Tobin LeJeune, it just so happens that I love you, too."

- - -

"You know in all the time we were together, this is the first time I've ever driven your truck," she says.

"Yeah, well, don't get used to it. It's never going to happen again," I mumble. She grinds the gears as she slows down to stop at a stop sign. I feel like I'm going to be sick. It has little to do with Delia's poor driving of a standard, but that isn't helping either.

"It's this one up here on the left," I say smugly.

"I know which—" She stops and looks at me. "Oh, I see. You're trying to be funny."

She pulls the truck into the driveway and then starts toward the front door.

"Okay, so, I'm going to call Weston, and then get you inside."

The mention of his name makes me fume with anger. She speaks softly into the phone like it's too private for me to hear. I wonder what she's telling him. I can't focus enough on anything to concentrate on her voice right now.

"I don't need your help," I say after she hangs up.

She's wearing that same damn pair of cut offs that she always did, the ones that always drove me a little crazy. I want to run my finger along the frayed edges. I shouldn't be thinking about things like that right now, but I am. "Tobin, I'm not leaving you out here."

"Whatever," I say. "So, isn't your boyfriend going to be pissed that you're with me?"

Delia lightly tiptoes up the stairs.

"And where are you going?" I ask.

"I'm going to make sure you get settled in bed. You really need to get some rest. Oh, and for the record, Weston isn't your concern," she says.

"Ah, that's sweet. I didn't think you had it in you to stand up for anything," I say. She turns around with eyes narrowed; she opens her mouth like she wants to say something, but lets it snap shut. The thought of getting her all riled up is so damn hot. I take my time going up the stairs, because I'm not entirely sure that they aren't going to slip out from under me.

"Tobin, don't do this, I'm just trying to help," she says. She holds the bedroom door open for me. I should be worried about waking my parents, but Dad would never interfere and waking Mom would be like waking the dead with all of the medication she's taking.

"So, when exactly did you decide you were over me and start sleeping with the captain of the polo team?" I ask.

She drops the pillow that she had been fluffing onto my bed and grits her teeth. I sort of love seeing her pissed off.

"That's not how it was and you know it," she says through clenched teeth.

I close the bedroom door behind me. The fact that she doesn't deny that they are sleeping together tears at me.

"Then tell me how it *was*, Delia. Here's your chance. You're free to say it all. Shit, I won't even remember it in the morning!" I laugh.

"We can talk about this when you're sober, Tobin."

I hear a car idling down on the street. That was fast. He must have one of those fancy GPS things to have found the house so quick. And maybe he doesn't like the idea of her here with me.

"So, I'm gonna go. Get some sleep, and I'll see you tomorrow," she says. She stares at me briefly then just turns and leaves. Like it's so easy for her. Why can't it be that easy for me?

I hear the front door open downstairs and I just can't let it go like that. I haul ass down the stairs, slipping on the last three and almost break my neck.

"D!" I call out the door.

She spins on her heels and I notice the Ralph Lauren model is standing at the passenger side door, ready to open it for her. He looks up at me, and I can't tell from his expression what he does or doesn't know about me. I really don't care at this point.

"Why?" I demand.

She raises her finger to Weston to signal that she'll just be a minute and starts back toward me, hands on her hips, shaking her head.

"Why what, Tobin?"

"Why did you leave me like that? Why did you run off with someone else so fucking fast?" I'm slurring my words a little. I can hear it, but I can't stop.

"I didn't leave you, Tobin. Don't be absurd. You know what, I can't do this right now, and *you* shouldn't want to. It doesn't matter anymore," she says.

And I wish to God that it didn't, but it does. Because the last time anything was okay was when Delia was in my life and at our house for Sunday dinner and Eamon was there and my mom was awake and it just *all* matters.

"Everything okay, sweets?" Weston is here now and I don't want him this close to her. Or me.

"Everything is fine. You can go back to your car," I tell him.

"It's fine, Weston, I can take care of myself," she says.

I snort. "Since when?"

Weston hasn't moved. Instead, he holds Delia's hand and I want to pummel him for it.

"Why don't I just get you home," he says to her.

She nods and starts to walk away with him. *Your hand in mine.*

And I snap.

"Okay, D. I hope you find whatever it is that you're looking for. Or whatever it is that your dad is looking for, for you. You're a fucking mess!" I yell after her.

I expect Ralph Lauren to come back after me, but he doesn't. Instead, Delia is in my face. Staring at me with intensity I've never seen in her before. Even in my drunken haze, I can see the anger ignite in her eyes

"I know you're drunk. And grieving. But fuck you, Tobin."

I've never heard her swear like that. I've never seen her *passionate* about something like that.

"Shit, I want to kiss you right now," I say.

"Don't you dare. Go to bed. I'm leaving. *With my boyfriend.* You go and sober up." She's leaving again.

And this time, I have to let her go.

WHAT IS SAFE?

Is safe the hands that hold you no matter what?
Or is safe someone hurting enough to fight?

Is safe the one who is strong as a pillar?
Or is safe who wants to use the strength of two, not
one?

Is love safe?
Or is it better to find comfort?
Can there be comfort without love?
Can passion come from warmth?
Or does it need to come from fire?

14

Delia

I rest my head against the cold window as I count the bright streetlights on the way back to my house. I know exactly how many there are. Fifty-two between his house and mine. I know because the last time I drove away from Tobin's house, concentrating on counting them was the only thing that kept me from crumbling.

I'm in the car with Weston. It's over. We're gone, and Tobin's hopefully sleeping it off. Damn him. *Shit, I want to kiss you right now.* What the hell!

The scariest thing is that if Weston hadn't been there...I might...no. Not Tobin. Too late. *Way* too late.

It's a relief to not be in that house anymore— weighed down with grief. There are too many memories, and too many of them good. How many times did I sit with him, his parents and Eamon playing cards at the kitchen table? How many pitchers of sweet tea did his mom and I share on the front porch while I waited for Tobin to get home from work? Too many to just forget, that's for sure.

I sigh and slump even lower in the seat. It feels like I had to call Weston to come rescue me, which sucks because that's what he's always done for me. I knew he wouldn't be mad, because he loves the role. I did lie and tell him I got lost when I stumbled onto Tobin—like I could get lost in these woods.

"I'm sorry. I know this is totally awkward." I let my eyes find Weston's profile in the dim light of the car. There's no way for me to not be completely embarrassed by Tobin's outburst, and I'm wondering if Weston's getting too good of a look at the little country girl making her way in D.C. Will he start to wonder who I am? 'Cause that one's hitting me right now.

I'm waiting for some lecture, or for him to say how weird this is, or how totally inappropriate it was of me to help Tobin home.

Weston's hand reaches across the car to take mine. "It *is* awkward, but I understand, at least a little."

I'm shocked. "You're not mad?"

"The way he talked to you upset me, and I was a little surprised at how you answered." He sounds a little like my dad, but I let it slide because I can't believe that he isn't pissed.

"But you're not mad at me?" I realize as I ask that I almost want him to be. I want him to be mad that instead of sneaking into his room, I snuck outside. Tobin would have been pissed—well, because he'd have been hurt.

"Did you sneak out and plan to meet with him?" Even a corner of his mouth pulls up. He is actually, really, seriously, not mad.

"No."

"Did you kiss him?"

"No."

"He's your friend, Delia. You have history. You helped him out. I'm not mad." His thumb brushes the top of my hand, and his eyes are all sincerity.

Grandma's words slip into my head—make love with the same passion as you argue. But what if you don't argue? Even over the big things? This seems pretty big.

There's more to Weston than I give him credit for. And it's the stupidest thing in the world for me to feel split between a guy I still feel betrayed by, and Weston—who is sometimes exactly what I'd expect, and is sometimes so much more. I have to do something to thank him.

"Stop the car."

"What?" he asks.

"Pull over." I let the corner of my mouth turn up. If I can get Weston to make me feel like Tobin makes me feel—only without all the hurt and games…

A faint smile passes across his lips, as he turns down a small side street and pulls over.

I kiss him softly, and his mouth immediately opens like he's trying to devour me. I wonder if this is what happens to guys when they don't have sex—like all the other stuff needs to be bigger, more intense.

"Slow down," I whisper as I pull away from his kiss.

"What?" He's already out of breath but pauses.

"You just…" I need to open my mouth and say it. Tell him what I want.

Weston backs away.

I reach out for his hands. This is the guy who saved me when I first got to D.C. The guy who made all the photo-op stuff Dad wanted me to be a part of bearable. Because not every senator's kid is tortured the way I am.

Why aren't I feeling more?

"What?" He's looking at me with confusion. Of course he is. I never ask for anything.

"Never mind. I'm sorry." I pull on his hand, but he leans away.

"What's going on?" His brows pull together.

I stare at the seat between us. *Okay. Deep breath. Get it out.* "I want to slow down when we're together. Take more time. I—"

His fingers touch my chin, bringing my face level with his. His lips brush mine softly, sending a wave of shivers through me. My eyes close.

Tobin's there.

No, no, no. Tobin does *not* get to be in this moment, again. He also doesn't get to make me feel bad about this moment.

I part my lips, and Weston's still hovering, just close enough to me that I can feel his smile on my lips. His fingers touch the side of my face, slide down my arms, and rest on my shoulders where he starts drawing patterns.

Slow.

It's all things that should make my knees weak, and my heart pound faster, and it sort of does, but I'm only half here, and I don't know how to bring the rest of myself into what should be an amazing moment between us. I was right earlier—if I just told Weston what I want, he'd try.

Now I'm thinking that I was wrong when I thought Weston was like my dad. So wrong. Weston's good, and kind, and still kissing me so softly.

"I love you, Delia," Weston whispers as he touches me.

I put my arms tightly around him, pressing our bodies together in the confines of the car. And that same comfort that's always been a part of him wraps me up even tighter than his arms.

"I'm sorry you lost your friend." His hand strokes my hair.

I break down in tears, once again not even sure how much of it is about Eamon, and how much is me going slowly insane back in this town.

I have no words for Weston, only confusion. About everything. Weston only knows the girl I've tried to be. Tobin knows the girl I really am. The one who'd read nothing but poetry all day long. The girl who half-lives on sweet tea, and goes barefoot, even on the rocks. Weston knows the manicured Delia. What would he think of the real girl?

"It's okay, Delia. I'm here." His fingers gently wipe away my tears, leaving me with even more guilt in their place.

His words make me cry harder, because there's no denying anymore that Weston feels more than I do, and a horribly selfish part of me is using him. I don't want to just use him. I want the passion of Tobin with the safeness of Weston. Something I'm starting to realize is completely impossible.

Why haven't I trusted Weston with all the parts of me? I trusted Tobin, and I still love him for it. Maybe still more than I love Weston. I love and hate admitting this to myself.

I wonder if there's any way I can make Weston enough for me to not feel Tobin anymore. Probably there is. It almost feels like there has to be.

Enough is a dangerous word.

I was never able to do enough for my father, and I'm beginning to wonder if Weston would ever be enough for me. Maybe I want him to be, and that's all I need.

ENOUGH

Enough is impossible
There's no way to fill it
No way to see it.
No way to live up to it.

It is simply the measure we use
When we want to say
You're just not what I want
And probably never will be

15
Tobin

The sounds of daylight come way too early. My head feels foggy and swollen from the six-too-many beers I had last night. I rub my jaw; I really need to shave. I'm probably looking as rough as I feel right now. This is the morning of my brother's funeral and look at me—*I'm* the one that's a fucking mess. There was one other time that I remember feeling so disgusted with myself.

Eamon had left me laid out on the front lawn, lying there on the wet grass, drunk but happy. The sky was full of spinning stars above me. It was beautiful. He'd gone to follow Delia home and make sure she got back into the house okay. I normally walked her home through the woods, but I'd celebrated a little too much that night on account of it being my birthday.

Delia made Eamon promise to stay and get me in the house safely and not to do anything stupid. But as soon as she left, I made him break that promise by leaving to keep an eye on her. He assured me she'd never even notice he was there, because if she did, she would've been pissed that he left me.

It wasn't the first time I'd had him check up on her. I knew it was my job, but Eamon was a good alternative in a pinch. He joked with Delia incessantly, but I knew he'd do anything for her because she was important to me.

I was content staring up at the sky until he got back. If I closed one eye, I could make everything stop spinning long enough to make out the Summer Triangle. That's another thing that Eamon taught me—stars. He learned them from our granddad, but I never knew him. He passed before I was old enough to remember him at all. And then the sky came to an abrupt halt. Mr. Gentry was hovering above me with his hair gelled flat to his head, shirt tucked tightly into his pants and a stern look on his face.

I hauled myself off of the ground as fast as I could and extended my hand to shake his, but he ignored it.

"Delia's not here," I said, shoving my hands into my pockets.

"I'm well aware. I waited to come until I heard her sneak back into the house. Nice of you not to even see her home, being as you're the reason for her ridiculous behavior lately," he said. His voice was controlled, but anger crept around each word.

"Okay..." I said. Then what the hell are you doing here, is what I wanted to say.

"You two think you're being so sneaky that I haven't noticed her absence at night. I'm not a stupid man, Tobin—unlike my daughter, who seems to have lost all common sense since she met you. Delia has an incredible future in front of her, and the absolute only thing standing in her way is you. I intend to put a stop to that right now."

"Sir, with all due respect, I'm not sure I understand. I completely support Delia in whatever she wants to do," I said.

He made a sound that sounded like *"tisk tisk"* with his tongue, and I honestly wanted to punch him right then.

"How exactly, Tobin, do you think you can support anything that she does? What do you do? You're a welder, right? That isn't going to put her through college and then medical school."

I didn't realize this confrontation was about money, though I should have figured. I didn't make a fortune, but it would enough to live a good life and someday, support a small family off of. My dad always managed to take care of us, at least.

"Yes sir, but Delia has never mentioned medical school. I'm not sure that's what she's got planned—"

He was quickly in my face. I'd had a lot to drink, and my judgment wasn't the greatest right then. I held my breath, willing him to back off before I ended up in jail.

"Delia has got plans of whatever I say her future will hold. You are nothing but trash, an insignificant blip in what will otherwise be a stellar life for her. She will have everything she deserves, Tobin, and you son, are not it."

I could feel his breath on my face. I allowed myself the briefest of seconds to consider his words before I felt myself being pushed backward.

It wasn't Mr. Gentry, but Eamon. He stood in between us, pushing us both away from each other.

"What seems to be the problem, Mayor?" He smiled at Delia's father, but I knew that look. He was trying to help me out, but wondering what the hell I'd done.

"You boys both stay away from my Delia," he said. "I don't want to have this conversation again, Tobin. You know you're no good for her."

When he'd left in his shiny Cadillac, Eamon punched me in the arm.

"What the fuck did you do this time?" he asked.

"He doesn't want me to see Delia anymore," I said.

"I fucking told you that would happen. Is she really worth all this trouble, bro?"

I nod. She was worth it for me, but I wondered sometimes if I was worth it for her. "Did she get home okay?"

Eamon rolled his eyes.

"Of course she did. I told you I'd make sure," he said. "So, what'd Newt Gingrich have to say?"

"I'm not good enough for her. I'll never be able to

take care of her the way she deserves." *All true,* I wanted to add.

Eamon scoffed. "Bro, don't buy that shit. He just doesn't want to accept that his little girl doesn't need him anymore. You take good care of her, you love her, and for some stupid reason she loves your country ass, too. It'll work out," he said.

"And if he stands in the way? I don't want to make her life hard because of me."

"Oh, he's going to stand in the way, but you knew that going into it. And when shit hits the fan, I'll be here for you, just like I always am." He punched my arm again, "Come on, lets get your scurvy ass inside."

- - -

I never told Delia about that visit from her dad, and it wasn't our last run-in. I *did* make her life difficult, in every way possible. If I wasn't so damn selfish, I probably would've let her go a long time ago. I always thought that if D and I could have just locked ourselves away from the outside world, that we'd be okay. We could last forever. But that wasn't realistic. And after last night, I doubt I had to worry about her ever so much as speaking to me again. She'd seen me drunk plenty of times, but I'd never acted out toward her.

My phone buzzes on the nightstand next to me.

I'm bringing Weston today. I hope you understand.

Honestly, I can't blame her. She sees stupid drunk every day with her mom, I'd always been so careful to never cross that line in front of her and last night, I'd done it. She *does* deserve better. I hope she's found it with Weston.

I sit up too quickly and the pressure in my head makes me dizzy. I chug what's left of a bottle of water on my nightstand and pop the cap off a bottle of Advil. It's empty. It's going to be a fucking gold-star day, I can tell already.

The thing I wonder most often is if I should even bother writing my thoughts down.
Who would want to hear from a spoiled daughter of an asshole for a senator?
And who would want to read poems, from a country girl?

16

Delia

I lie completely still in bed. Maybe if I don't move, it will make today not real. Normally, when Weston sleeps over, I make sure I'm downstairs good and early to do something for breakfast. It doesn't happen often, but last night was not the first night that Dad had allowed Weston to stay the night.

No way he'd have allowed that with Tobin. The only time Tobin managed to stay over was when Gram died, and all he did was hold me. Well, and Dad was out of town, and I'm sure Mom never told him.

My eyes rest on my bookshelf. I still haven't moved.

Nothing but poetry. Eamon gave me such crap over that. I'd read *Leaves of Grass* ten times over in one summer, and he stole that book from me more times that I could count. He'd start to read in a ridiculous voice, and at first I'd try and jump up to catch it, and then I learned that if I was patient enough, he'd get bored and give it back.

Tobin got it, just like he got everything about me. No one but grandma asked why my bookshelves were filled with poetry. But Tobin understood; even let me read to him, even though it had to be against some LeJeune boy's code for poetry to be read out loud. Tobin gave me a book for it after my surgery, a leather journal I still have.

Something to write in.

They won't all be good, but I know you have it in you, Delia, I love you.

I've wanted to rip that page out so many times, but I can't, and now I'm so glad I didn't.

My grandmother was the one who got me interested in poetry. Whenever I would come home sick from school, I'd go to her house. She would set me up with a nice fluffy pallet on the sofa using squishy down pillows and soft quilts that had been passed down on her side of the family.

She'd make me hot cocoa—the real stuff, not from a cheap packet and read me poetry. Not all classics, some serious, some silly—all wondrous. I loved how you could say things in a poem—even simple, mundane things and they sounded beautiful, important. Writing poetry gave me the courage to acknowledge my thoughts. It made them valid. Real.

I actually think Tobin started to love it too, or maybe he loved me enough that he understood.

Enough about Tobin.

If last night wasn't enough to show that he and I have nothing left, I don't know what is. We'll be lucky if we can salvage a *friendship* after the mess we've dug ourselves into.

I can't believe we're burying Eamon today. I blink and a few soft tears hit the pillow. Damn him for being so stubborn and thinking he was invincible.

It makes me wonder if Tobin was sitting in the place where Eamon died. I hope not. That was our spot on the tracks.

"Okay, Delia," I say to myself. "Stop. You can try to salvage a friendship, but now is not the time. Let's just get through our day. You know how to get through a day. One foot in front of the other, one smile over another. You can do it."

And this is when I'm thankful for Weston. He knows how to get me through days like today, and not only does he get me through them, but he wants to be there for me. It's why I fell in love with him. There isn't room in my heart for two boys—I'm too stretched out already.

I've got to let Tobin go.

I wander downstairs in my pajamas, throwing a black tank over my white one so I don't need to mess with a bra. My face is clean, my hair is down, and it feels amazing.

"Morning." Mom's sleepy eyes don't even glance my way from her favorite chair on the porch beyond the kitchen.

I wonder if her and Dad made up, or if they're back to their quiet politeness. I'm waiting for her to say something about last night.

"You're welcome to have one." She gestures to the counter.

"A Bloody Mary?" I can feel my eyebrows pull up as disbelief sets in.

"Why not? You're practically married to a politician. You need it." She takes another long drink, and I start to wonder if Mom remembers last night when she waved me out the door.

I grab the counter and lose my breath. Is she right? No. She isn't right. I'm not married to Weston. I'm barely graduated from high school. I haven't even picked a major yet, and it surely won't be anything to do with politics.

But he might as well be.

I grab Mom's mix and pour a large glass before taking a seat near her to look out across the empty lawn. "I'm not married to Weston."

Mom gives me this odd look over her drink. "You know you're a half-step from it. He's talked with your father."

I spit half my drink out, and my heart's hammering so hard I'm not sure if I'll hear her answer. *"He's what?"*

"Who's what?" Dad laughs as he steps onto the porch, and then frowns as he catches sight of my drink.

"Don't start," Mom says, gesturing loosely with her hand. "It was my idea."

Dad lets out a frustrated breath. "I'm going to hit the golf course while I'm here, see what old Mickey's up to. Maybe get a few swings in before the funeral this afternoon."

"Fine." Mom's voice has the apathetic, quiet quality it nearly always has – except when she puts her foot down about something and she and Dad have it out.

Dad glances at my attire. "For God's sake, Delia. Clean yourself up."

I open my mouth to argue, but remember that the new Delia is strictly forbidden from speaking up. Not that I ever did much of it before, but after we left Crawford, and Dad buried my secret—*our secret*, it was very much enforced.

Weston's hands touch my shoulders and then run down my arms. "I don't have to go," he whispers onto my bare shoulder. "I came here to be with you. I'm sure your dad will survive without me."

"Go." I nod.

He softly kisses the side of my face. "I want you to be sure."

"I'm sure." I pat his hands, and catch Mom doing the same thing to Dad out of the corner of my eye. My stomach flips over. *I'm my mother.* I don't want to be my mother.

"You're the best." He kisses my cheek again before pushing away.

"We okay?" Dad asks.

"My girl says its fine." Weston gives Dad a wink, and I want to throw my glass against the wall.

They start talking golf before they've even stepped into the garage. Weston came for a funeral. *One where they're burying a friend of mine.* And now he's going to play golf.

"Don't break the glass." Mom gestures to me before taking another drink.

I'm clutching my cup of Bloody Mary so tight my fingers ache. "I'm going for a walk."

Mom nods in understanding, but I'm pretty sure she's already had a couple re-fills on her drink. "Clean yourself up a little first, Delia. You're a mess."

There are very few things that grate me more than Dad's words echoed in something Mom says. Instead of making a fuss, I down the rest of the Bloody Mary, and head upstairs to "clean up."

A shower, blow-dry, and a clean outfit later—tiny blue shorts with a silk top—I'm headed back downstairs.

Mom's still in her housecoat in the kitchen when I sit to buckle my wedge sandals.

"You forgot your makeup." She gestures to my clean face as she moves out of the room with her drink.

"Thank you, Mom." Hopefully she won't say anything else. I can't imagine wearing makeup in this heat. And suddenly I'm not sure if I'm going anywhere or not. Today is Eamon's funeral.

My chest cracks again.

∽

"Why don't you like me?" I asked Eamon after Tobin and I had been together a few months. Eamon was nice enough, but it felt forced, and I swear all he knew how to do with me was tease.

"I like you just fine, Delia." He planted a wet kiss on my cheek.

"Gross, Eamon." I shoved him away as I laughed.

He stepped outside, where I'd been waiting for Tobin to come home from work. He was running late like he often did—Tobin hated leaving a project half-done.

"Eamon. I'm serious." I followed him into the yard.

"And so am I, Miss Priss."

"See!" I threw my hands in the air. "That's what I'm talking about!"

He sighed as he threw a leg over his dirt bike and reached for his helmet.

"Do you think I'm not good enough for him?"

"Nope. Not that poor bastard." Eamon chuckled. "He's lucky he can get anyone to notice him."

"Then what is it?"

"I got no problems with you, Delia. You're pretty cool for a spoiled, rich girl."

"Uh…" I wanted to throw an insult back at him, but wasn't sure what to say.

"It's not you. It's the whole idea of someone as young as him, and especially as young as you, attaching themselves like y'all are doing. I think it's stupid, and it sucks because when it all goes to hell between you two, I'll be the one to pick up the pieces because that boy is gone over you." Eamon put on his helmet.

"I'd never…" I shook my head, but Eamon had already started his bike and took off down the road.

I heard Tobin blare the horn on his truck just before he pulled into the driveway.

His smile at seeing me dropped every bit of tension Eamon just added on.

"There's my girl!"

And I jumped into his arms.

- - -

"Delia!" Dad's voice almost catapults me out of my chair on the porch. "What on *earth* were you thinking?"

"What?" I didn't realize so much time had passed and that Dad and Weston were back already.

"Don't *what* me." Dad sits on a chair next to me, and leans in my direction.

I want to set my jaw and look him straight in the eye, but instead I shrink back into the seat and stare at my hands. I'm really starting to hate this side of me. Emails asking my friends for time are one thing. Facing my father is another. Just his tone makes my body shake.

"Where's Weston?" Anyone to save me from whatever Dad has to say.

"He's getting ready. Which you should be doing, too. You look like damn hippie in that blouse." He scowls.

I glance down at the silk. This blouse cost my dad over three hundred dollars at Neiman Marcus, and I want to laugh.

"Weston told me about last night."

My stomach turns over, and I pull in a slow, deep breath to try and keep from shaking. I finger the hem of my blouse and wonder if there's anything I could say to get me out of this.

"I thought we'd left this alone, Delia. If what you had to do didn't teach you to stay away from that boy, I don't know *what* to do for you." There's a hardness, and a mean, almost sarcastic edge to his voice. "Or if anything can be done."

"But—" Dad needs to know how it all happened.

"Keep your mouth shut when I'm talking, Delia." His steely eyes don't leave mine.

I'm blinking back tears, and biting my lip, trying to just wait it out.

"Weston is the best kind of boy. He loves you more than you'll ever find from anyone else. His dad has all but sealed up my election this fall, and if he's ready to forgive you for not only your past, but your damn little stunt last night, then you better grab him while you can, because not many decent boys would want someone who—"

"Dad, I don't think you understand what happened. I just went for a walk. I didn't think I'd run into anyone! It's that—"

"Delia!" He barks, silencing me and spilling the tears down my cheeks. "Let's not add *liar* to the long list of sins stacked against you. This is my final warning to you. Understand?"

I clutch my stomach and nod.

"Now." He stands up, a painted smile on his face. "Let's get prettied up, and put on our best smiles, okay?"

"Okay," I say, hating myself a little more than I thought possible.

"Delia, I'm sorry," Weston whispers as I knot up my hair.

His face is pleading as he stands just outside my bathroom. My bedroom door is politely open.

"It's fine." I take another breath and blink away a few more tears as I stare at my reflection in the mirror. I pull up another strand of hair and grab a bobby pin. "It's not like I was going to escape today without crying."

As I look at my face in the mirror, I know that Eamon would give me hell over how my hair was pulled up too tight, and he'd hate that Weston is here. Right now *I* hate that Weston is here. Sending a text to Tobin was a stupid coward move, but better than him not know Weston's coming at all.

There's no way to tell Weston not to come now. How do I say that I can't hurt the brother of the deceased?

Screw it. Dad's already pissed. I jerk out the pins and let my hair fall.

Weston sighs. "He asked about the car because he heard me either leave or come back in, or—"

Wait. At first I was mad just because he told Dad I rescued Tobin. My chest drops.

"Oh no, you didn't get in trouble, too, did you?"

He looks away, like he doesn't want to say.

I stand and face Weston, suddenly tense and wondering what happened between them. "What did he say?"

Weston's eyes come back to mine. "He gave me a wink and said something about you and I taking off together. I didn't want him to think that of me." His voice falters. "Of *us*, I mean, so I told him that you'd gone for a walk and needed to be picked up." He runs his hands over the front of his black suit a few times.

So, that's how Dad got the whole story. "And I imagine he knows why and where, and…" *everything*. I'm nodding without meaning to, feeling sick that Dad will be thinking—typical Tobin, even though he just lost his brother. I know Tobin partied less when he and I were together. He was careful. Always careful with me until the end. I'd been around enough to know that. Dad just never gave him the chance.

And now Weston covered for himself by using Tobin, which was all true, so it's not fair of me to pin that on him, either.

"I'm sorry, Delia. I really am." His whole face and body and everything is so pleading.

I sigh and turn away. "Damn hypocrite," I say under my breath as I turn toward the mirror, my hair falling around my face. I've put on makeup, but just a touch. Almost nothing. And my hair's staying down.

"Delia?"

"My father, not you."

I open my mouth to tell him that I'd just gotten a lecture on what a sinner I am, but Dad's apparently winking at Weston over his own daughter. The thing is— Weston and I haven't talked about my past. I dumped everything from the old Delia and left it in Crawford. The problem is that now I'm back, and the two parts of my life don't seem as compatible as I thought they might be.

"I shouldn't have said anything, Delia. I'm really sorry."

"It's not you." I sigh. *It's my dad. It's me. It's Tobin.*

Weston steps close to me and slides his arms around my waist. "It'll get better."

I lean in and let him think he's comforting me, but my dad isn't getting better, he's getting worse, and I don't know how much more stress I can take.

17

Tobin

The church is still decorated from a wedding the night before. I find this both completely appalling and amusing. The guy who was always most likely to never get married had ended up in a church full of carnations, bows and baby's breath.

"Tobin." Dad nudges me. Shit, they're all waiting on me to speak. I don't even have to look over my shoulder to know that everyone in the church is staring. I can feel their empathetic eyes trained on me.

I make my way to the pulpit. I button my suit jacket and straighten my tie. I had a time trying to get it just right this morning. Whenever we had a wedding or other event to go to, Delia always did that for me.

She stood back to look at me in my suit.

"I sort of like seeing you dressed up like this." Delia smiled wide.

"Yeah, well, don't get used to it. I feel like a freak in this thing," I said. "Tell me again why we have to go to this?"

She frowned.

"Tobin, you promised. If I went to your family's

Cochon de Lait last weekend, you'd come to my dad's fundraiser with me. Now, let me fix your tie. I think a half-Windsor will look better with this collar than a Four-in-Hand."

I rolled my eyes because I had no idea what the difference was.

"That's different. Roasted pig is good. Hanging out with a bunch of suits is bad." I tried to laugh so she'd take it as sarcasm, but I was pretty serious. Going to these country club functions was my least favorite thing about being with Delia. I didn't fit in. I had nothing to offer in conversations, and I actually had to buy a suit for the first time in my life.

"Besides, your dad doesn't want me there." I waited a brief moment for her to deny that, but she didn't.

"That's true," she said. She untied my tie and then worked to perfect the knot, her brows pulled together in concentration. "But, he thinks I won't put on a happy face if he doesn't let you come, so he's bending his own rules for tonight. There." She smoothed the tie down and stood back to admire her work. "It looks much better like that, right?"

"Right," I agreed. I honestly couldn't tell the difference between the two.

"All right, we'd better get going," she said, checking her watch.

"Sure I can't entice you into getting out of that dress and staying in?" I asked. I pulled her in by her waist, my thumbs finding her hip bones that I loved so much. I pressed my mouth to her neck and she let out a content sigh. My lips moved across her chest and I picked up her dainty arm and kissed the length of it.

By the way she was responding to me, I thought for a second she might actually agree to stay home. But she swatted my hand away just as I reached around to the back of her form fitting, sparkling black dress and gave the zipper a light tug.

"Come on, you know we can't do this right now. My dad will go crazy if I don't show up!"

"I'm about to go crazy," I said. "I need you." I let out an involuntary growl and tried to shake it off.

"What you *need* is a cold shower," she joked.

"I'll settle for a swim after we get this over with," I told her.

"Deal." She reached out and shook my hand in agreement.

- - -

Always a trade. Always a compromise. Until there wasn't anything left to bargain with, because neither one us had any clue what to do. If it had been just the move, we might have been able to deal.

I shake the memory. It wasn't the place to be thinking about that night.

I sort of fucked up, because I don't have anything written down. Not a single word. I tried several times this morning, sitting in Eamon's jeep outside of the church. I just couldn't put what Eamon was and what he meant to me in words that these people sitting here would understand. All while keeping the swearing to a minimum. It was too much to ask of anyone, and for a second, I'm angry at my mom for making me do this.

I lean onto the podium and sigh. The entire church is full. Each seat occupied with some dark dress or suit, and several people standing against the back wall. I clear my throat. I've never liked talking in front of people, and with Eamon's flower-draped casket next to me, I like it even less. My nerves are so shot that I can't even make out people's faces. I guess that makes the fact that I have no clue what I'm going to say a little easier. I open my mouth, and then shut it again, reasoning that no one here cares that Eamon's favorite food was rice pudding, or that he could drink any person here under the table.

I stare into the rows of people one last time, and that's when I see her. In a sea of faceless blurs, Delia is there. She nods at me encouragingly. She believes in me. That simple nod brings the words up through my throat.

"When I was seven and Eamon was ten, we decided we wanted to run away and live out in the woods. I don't really remember why we thought to do that. Mom and Dad weren't so bad, so it wasn't anything like that." I let out a small, stiff laugh and a few others in the church follow suit.

"We got a big backpack and stockpiled bottles of water and food for weeks. We'd take little things here and there so that Mom and Dad wouldn't notice. We must have had four gallons of water in that damn—err, darn pack." I don't exactly know where to go with this story, but for whatever reason, of all of the ridiculous stunts Eamon and I pulled over the years, this was the first one to pop into my head. I wipe my sweaty palms on my slacks and start again. "We waited until Mom and Dad had both left for work and then ran into the woods. We set up a makeshift camp. We pitched our small tent, started a little fire and spent the day wandering the banks of the creek.

"I decided to climb some trees and somehow, I lost sight of Eamon along the creek. It got dark shortly after and I knew that I needed to get back to our camp. I didn't have any water, or a jacket or anything. It didn't take me long to realize that I was lost. I don't know how long I walked in circles before Eamon found me.

"I knew he was going to be mad. He had told me to stay right by him. I heard him running up behind me, yelling my name and I thought for sure he was going to give me a beating, but instead, he hugged me. I know kids, especially boys don't do that, but Eamon did.

"He never had any trouble letting people know how he really felt. I asked him why he came looking for me, why he didn't just go and get Mom and Dad. He told me, *"Because I'm your brother. Brothers don't leave each other wandering around in the dark alone, Tobin."*

I finally blink and break Delia's stare.

"And you know what? He proved that to me over and over again. He was always there for me. He was there for all of us. It might never have been his official job to protect me, or any of us, but it was one he never slacked on, and I was proud to be his brother.

"He taught me important things, like how to build the best possible fort in the attic, using every blanket and sheet in the house. He taught me how to clean a gun, how to change the oil in the car, and more importantly, how to take care of the people that you love.

"When he got older, he was the definition of work hard, play hard. He'd go out with you boys and cause all sorts of mayhem," I said, pointing at Traive, Nelson and Eamon's other group of friends. They all nodded and smiled.

"He'd play as hard as he could, filling his nights with laughter and good friends. And after three hours of sleep, he'd leave you all sprawled out, and go to work, or help my parents around the house.

"A few years ago, when Dad got hurt at work,

Eamon didn't give it a second thought that he'd pick up some extra shifts to help out. It was just never a question. That's what you did for family.

"And last year, when I had my first lesson in having my heart trampled on." I don't dare look up and see Delia's reaction. "He was there. He was there when I didn't know what to do, how to get out of bed in the morning and move on, or how to make sense of any of it.

He was *always* there.

"I've never had anyone this close to me die before." The tightness in my throat is growing, burning. "The last few days have been really hard. Really dark and confusing and lonely for me. I don't know how to process all that's happened, how to accept that Eamon isn't going to pop into my room in the morning with some new scheme that he wants me in on. Losing him has really made me take stock in my life, to take measure of who I am, and who I want to become. I haven't figured all of those things out just yet, but I know that I'm not alone while I do. I know that Eamon is right here alongside me. Because brothers don't let each other wander in the dark alone."

I lower my eyes to the emerald green carpet and make my way back to my seat. It's over.

18

Delia

My heart aches, breaks, and then does it all over again. Like there is a fault line right down the center. A fracture that can't be healed. Because of Tobin. Because of Eamon. Because of everything and everyone that was lost. I wish I had some power to make Tobin feel better instead of worse. Thank God that Tobin had Eamon when we split. *Got his heart trampled on.* Sounds about right. Both of us. I never would have thought that either of us would have it in us to let each other go the way we did.

Part of me wants to be mad at Tobin. Mad at him for bringing me into this, but most of me just breaks. The church is filled with quiet, polite conversation. I'm still stunned into silence.

"Delia?" Weston whispers behind me.

Regret claws at my chest for a million things. For letting Weston come here with me. For letting Tobin go the way I did, because there's no fixing us now. That Eamon died, even though I couldn't have prevented that.

I glance around at the people I grew up with. The people who spread any news through town like their life depended on it. I smile as I wonder how many people discussed my coffee at the diner with Tobin and wonder who will challenge me next at shuffleboard bowling.

Weston's finger touches my cheek. "You're smiling and all teary. You okay?"

It takes everything in me not to jerk away from him. Something different starts to pour through me as I scan Weston's face. Nothing but concern on his features, in his eyes. I can't keep doing this, being with Weston, but I don't know how to stop.

The thing is—I don't know how much comfort I get from him touching me anymore, and that's not a good sign. Or maybe it's just the day and the surroundings.

"Come on," Dad says in his hushed whisper as his arms come around our shoulders, his political smile attached firmly in place. "Let's give our condolences so we can get out of here. I made reservations at the club tonight, and I'd like to go home and shower funeral off me before we go."

My jaw clenches at Dad's callousness. I glance back and Mom who also has her political face on. Hair perfectly smoothed, shaking hands, giving hugs, but I know her well enough to see that she's only half here. She's just had a lot more practice pretending than I have.

I'm numb.

I can't take it anymore—Dad's callousness, Mom's fakeness, and Weston's sweetness. I head for Tobin.

Unfortunately, a lot of people have gathered around the family.

"Wait, Delia." Weston's right behind me, but I'm not walking up to Tobin with Weston's arm on me.

I slide my way through until I'm face to face with him. Messy blond hair. Blue eyes. Everything I thought I'd look at forever, but now he's tired, weary. Grief is this black mask painted over him.

I don't want for Tobin to hold out his hand this time for a shake, and it doesn't matter that Weston is here with me. I slam into his chest as I put my arms around Tobin and hold on like he's the only thing that could keep me on the earth.

His arms come around me, low on my waist like always. Strong, like always. Protective, like always. I don't have to open my eyes to know his face is tilted down—I can feel his breath on my shoulder. His eyes are probably closed, and he's holding me every bit as tightly as I'm holding him.

I wonder if I can transfer my feelings through this hug. If somehow, he'll know how much I'm aching to be the one to comfort him.

We both breathe in at the same time. I don't know if we're breathing one another in, or if we're both trying not to cry.

"It was amazing, what you said," I whisper. "I love you."

Wait. Where did that come from? No. Wait. It's okay. Friends say I love you. I do love him. He's my youth, my growing up, how could I not?

I back away, but our eyes are now locked, so I only make it back a step. And then Weston's hand comes out to shake Tobin's. Seeing them touch brings a wave of nausea over me. Tobin's eyes only leave mine briefly to connect with Weston's, then come straight back to me.

Not only does Tobin hate me for good reason, I still think there's too much between us, but we might salvage something like friends.

Weston lightly rests his hand on my lower back as we walk away. I hate that I'm walking away with Weston's hand on me. I wish I could stand next to Tobin, his broken mother, and his father who's withering away to nothing.

It wasn't that long ago that I was considered part of his family. It wasn't that long ago that Tobin and I could have had our *own* family.

Instead I take a last look over my shoulder to see blue eyes staring back at me.

I'm wiped. I'm exhausted from Tobin, Weston, and the services. Everything. I'm still in my black dress, lounging on one of the chairs on the screened porch. Dad's upstairs washing "funeral" off of him, and I'm supposed to put on a happy face for our late dinner at the club. I hate those people.

Weston steps into the room and takes the lounge chair next to mine, but he doesn't lounge. He sits. Elbows on knees.

"I'm so stupid." Weston sighs.

"What are you talking about?" I shift my head to see him better.

"You and Tobin." He shakes his head. "Your dad told me everything, you know, earlier today, and I didn't care."

I'm not sure what to say. I'm shocked Dad told *anyone*. I'm like his big, dirty secret.

"You shouldn't have cared. It's all history."

"Some people would care that you'd been so *involved* with someone." His eyes widen, just a little.

"What? Having sex? Lots of people have sex before they're married, Weston." I'm not sure where he's going with this, but my heart's pounding because I'm probably not hiding how Tobin affects me very well.

"I thought I could marry you." His body shifts on his chair to face me.

"What?" Mom's words from that morning echo back to me. *He's talked with your father.*

"I mean, I wasn't sure, of course. But yeah. I've thought about it a lot." He slides his fingers together and stares at his hands for a moment.

It's starting to fall down around me—the life I've built up since leaving here. I should be sadder about it, but somehow, it comes as almost a relief. Weston's two years older than me. Twenty now. And still waiting for marriage, he told me.

One of the side effects of growing up with a pastor for a father—well, before he became a senator. It probably says something really special about him that he's willing to be with someone like me, or maybe it's just another matter of keeping up appearances, even with just me. It all goes to show that I'm afraid to trust anyone anymore.

I stare at his face. His smooth cheeks, soft lips, nice eyes. And I take back what I thought earlier. I don't think I would turn into my mother if I was with him, but could I be happier with someone else? Would Weston still love me if he knew I leaned over the bar in hopes a view of my cleavage would get me a beer, or would he be embarrassed for me? How would he feel if he knew that trading pieces of clothing and running around with muddy feet are some of my favorite things? That I read poetry and love it—only I've lost that girl and want her back.

Damn that Tobin. I've been begging myself to think it was just first love, but it's more than that. He gets me in places no one else does. Even if Weston tried, he wouldn't understand that sometimes stripping off your clothes and jumping in a black lake is the only way to end the day. That ragged cut-off shorts are the perfect thing to wear on nearly all summer days.

"I've lost you, haven't I?" he asks, his eyes taking me in just like I'm taking him in.

"I don't know anything right now." At least it's the truth.

Weston blinks a few times and sighs. "I don't want to *not* be with you, Delia."

I was a chicken and didn't want to be alone. What a crappy reason to be with someone. I'm sure if I was determined, I could forget about that. And also, we've had some great times together. Losing him feels horrible, but now, so does keeping him.

"I'm going out. I'll be right back." I stand. Needing air. Needing out. Away.

"Where are you going?" He sits up a little taller in his chair.

"I'm going to get some lemonade." Or just go for a drive. Or see if they're actually doing a bonfire tonight.

"I think we should talk." He stands to face me. "And we have dinner."

"When I get back?" I ask.

"Are you..." He glances down. "Are you meeting up with anybody?"

"Just ask if I'm meeting Tobin, Weston. And no, I'm not." I touch his arm, and I beg for that simple gesture to ease away all of my uncertainty, but it doesn't. It just makes me even more unsure than I already am.

Weston pulls me into a tight hug, and I feel everything between us. Until I started pulling away, everything with he and I was perfect. Or at least simple.

Maybe I was selfish to wish for anything more than that. I should probably be trying to get it back. But I'm not. I just don't have the energy right now.

I slide on my heels, and then kick them off in favor of my flip-flops, even though I'm still in my nice dress. I step outside without looking back. I don't want to know what Weston looks like right now. My best guess is that he will make some polite excuse for me, and he'll go to dinner with my parents without me. I'm sure I'm horrible for hoping this is the case.

But getting out will clear my head. It has to.

19

Tobin

She loves me. I can't believe she said that. What was I supposed to do, say it back? There, at the funeral? *Do* I still love her?

"Do you love me?" she asked.

"You know I do," I said. I reached over and pushed the tiny strap of her tank top off of her shoulder and pressed my lips to her hot skin. We'd been outside all day, riding four wheelers through the mud that a solid week of constant rain had left behind on our land. It was the first day of sunshine and Delia and I were taking advantage of it.

"Then you'll come tonight," she said.

"On his birthday? I just don't know if it's the best time."

Delia pulled on a light cotton button up shirt over her filthy tank top and left it unbuttoned. This was not what I expected when I first got involved with her. I didn't realize that under the prissy rich-girl (albeit gorgeous) exterior, was one of the most exciting, alive people I'd ever met. Someone who couldn't wait to see what every new day offered. At least when she was with me.

"Now is as good a time as any, Tobin. Besides, tonight it won't be so bad. My dad's side of the family will be on their best behavior so they don't offend Mom's side."

"Why is that?" I asked.

She laughed.

"Because Mom's side has the money."

I mulled this over for a second. "Wait, I thought your dad was loaded?"

She shook her head. "Nope. The house, the cars it all came from old money– *Mom's* money. Why do you think he's so desperate to hang on to everything?" She rinsed her hands in the hose, and then shocked me by taking a big drink from it.

"Come on, you filthy animal. Let's go inside and get a proper shower," I said.

"Tobin! Your parents may come home, I can't!" she said, but her smile said, *dare me.*

"Hey, if I'm going to this dinner tonight, I'm at least getting you naked first."

I slung her over my shoulder and ran toward the house with her squealing the entire way.

- - -

Its dusk by the time I get out of my house and pull up to the lake. There's a massive fire going and a sea of smiling people and red plastic cups. It feels good to be out of my house and all of the sadness. Mom and Dad were still visiting with out of town aunts and uncles when I said my goodbyes. I can't handle anymore today.

I did make a stop on the way here. Back to the cemetery. I noticed on my way out earlier that Delia's grandmother's grave didn't have any flowers. I'd been keeping it clean for the last year since they left town. I'd go out month or so and clean the headstone with soap and water and weed-eat to keep the brush from getting too overgrown. I'd leave a couple of flowers for her. Most of the time just daisy's from our yard, but every once in a while there would be a magnolia blossom on the tree at the end of our property that I'd catch at just the right time and bring for her.

No one noticed I did it, but that's not why I did. I don't even think I did it for Delia. I did it because it was the right thing to do for a lady who always saw in me what I hoped Delia's father someday would.

I reach inside the cab of the truck and start lugging the bags of ice I brought toward the row of ice chests.

"Let me help you," Delia says. She came out of nowhere.

"What are you doing here?" I ask.

"Same as you. Here to see some old friends and try to have a good time after today..." She doesn't finish her sentence. What else can you add to that, right?

"Where's the boyfriend?" The words come out before I can stop them.

"Um, he's out... With my dad."

She looks ashamed as she says the words. I almost feel bad for her. *Almost.*

"Right. Okay, well, have fun." I crack one of the ice chests open, rip a bag of ice and dump it in.

"Tobin, wait," she says. "Can we just like, talk?"

"About what, Delia? Look, I'm sorry about last night, really, but it's just not the time." I stare down at my feet. I'm not used to feeling like this. Exposed. Vulnerable.

"I mean, just, I'd like to explain about Weston being here and stuff. It wasn't my choice, really. I didn't even invite him down, it was my dad—"

I cut her off. "Right. It's always your dad, Delia. Let's just leave it alone." The day we buried Eamon is not the day to do this.

It *was* always her dad, though. Standing in the way. Like that night I came to see her after she'd had surgery and he wouldn't let me in the house. How different her relationship with Weston must be. To have her dad in their corner, I can't even imagine what that would have done for us.

꩜

"Tobin, you can't be serious." Mr. Gentry held the door open just enough to see who it was, but not enough to make me feel like there was any chance I'd be walking through it.

"I don't want to upset anyone, sir. I just want to check on her," I said.

"You know how I feel about you being near her at all. Did you really think by coming here I'd actually let you in my house?"

How had someone not kicked this man's ass before? Surely if someone had gotten him good like he deserved he wouldn't still be such a prick.

"She just had surgery. I need to be there—"

"Exactly. She just had surgery. That's yet another reason for you to stay away."

As if I had somehow caused her appendix to rupture. Add that to the list of things that were all my fault, huh? I was the one who'd taken her to the hospital when her dad told her to suck it up because they had photo's to take for his campaign.

Delia may have been tiny, but she wasn't weak. I'd rarely seen her cry, and never from physical pain. When she broke down at my house the other night, curled up in my lap, she couldn't even take a breath without sobbing, I rushed her to the hospital. She threw up in my truck and then again all over me as I carried her in through the sliding emergency room doors. And this asshole was telling me I couldn't see her?

Still, I wasn't going to cause a scene at his house. I wasn't going to risk upsetting Delia when she needed to rest. So I walked away. I was parked on the road. I knew Mr. Gentry would blow a gasket if I dared to park in his driveway.

I was just getting into my truck when Mrs. Gentry grabbed my arm. The smell of Amaretto hung heavily in the air. I'm surprised she put her drink down to come after me. She was a beautiful older woman, and that made me even sadder for her, the way her life was wasted with someone so awful.

"Tobin, I'm sorry that Randy was so ugly to you, but you had to know he wasn't going to let you come inside," she said.

"It was worth a shot. I had to try." I shrugged. "How is she?"

"Delia is doing fine. She's still very tired from the pain medicine that she's taking, but there were no problems with the surgery. She'll be good as new in a few days." She smiled at me and I realized how much Delia was her mother. They had the same warm smile that made you trust every word they said.

"Will you tell her that I came by?" I asked.

She nodded.

"And, can you give her this?" I handed Mrs. Gentry a small package. It was a book. A journal, actually. What next to no one, not even Mrs. Gentry, knew about Delia was that she loved poetry. She always had a book of poetry stashed in her purse.

Eamon would tease her about it, call her pretentious. She didn't mean to be. She said she just loved how simple words could be bent into something more, something beautiful. I asked her once why she didn't write her own. She laughed as if I'd just said the most unreasonable thing in the world. She said she couldn't. But I believed in her, and I knew that she could. I wanted her to *try*.

Mrs. Gentry glanced down at the wrapped book and sighed.

"Yes, Tobin, I'll give this to her. Now please, go on before he comes out and then we'll *both* be in trouble."

- - -

"Tobin, about what I said at the funeral, I—"

"It's fine." *I love you too*, is what I really want to say, but I can't. "Really, no explanation necessary. I'm sure your dad will be pissed if he finds out you're here talking to me anyway."

"Why do you always have to bring my dad into it?"

"Your dad is in it, he always has been. Holding you back. Making your decisions for you. Making you his little puppet," I say. The words should sting. I'm hoping. I want her to hurt. I shouldn't be the only one.

She laughs. A livid, phony laugh. "You, Tobin, are just as guilty of holding back as I am."

"What the hell are you even talking about?" I demand. I gave her everything I had.

"Eamon influenced you more than you thought. You knew how he felt about us—"

"Don't give me that crap. Eamon loved you. Don't you dare think otherwise." He did. He would've done anything for Delia, just like I would. She was family.

"I know that. He loved *me.* Not *us.* He wanted you to want what he did. To be just like him. I know how torn you were all the time, Tobin."

I slam the ice chest shut. She wants to have this out, let's do it.

"How can you stand here and act like there is nothing between us?" she asks.

"There isn't. Not to me at least. You left. You moved on. Pretty damn quickly, too."

"Are you kidding me? You weren't there. I had to make the hardest decision of my life. *Alone.* Moving on quicker than you seems like a small crime in comparison."

"In comparison?" I spit. "Are we keeping score now, D? Really?"

"You left me! You left me alone when I needed you the most!"

"I left you? I fucking lived and breathed for you, Delia," I say. She jerks back. Like the words bring her back to *us*. What we really were. Without all of this anger. It's the truth. "But because I didn't react the way that you wanted me to—"

"*Needed* you to. I *needed* you, Tobin," she qualifies. Her voice is cracking. Just like that night.

∽

"Tobin, I really need to talk to you," she said. Her voice was pleading, urgent.

"I work until six," I said. "I'll come by and pick you up when I get off."

"Oh, okay. Just get here as soon as you can." She was sniffling like she had been crying. Again. Shit. I was sure it was more drama over the move.

"Baby, are you okay?" I asked.

Silence.

"Do you need me to leave work early?" I really hoped she'd say no. It's not like I wasn't concerned about whatever was bothering her, but since we found out she was moving to D.C. next month, it seemed like everything was an emergency.

"So, are you going to tell me what's going on?" I asked later that night. She was sitting on the boat launch, her feet dangling just above the water. She hadn't looked up since we got here, and she was really starting to scare me. I'd never seen her like this.

"D?" I pressed.

"I need to tell you, but I also don't know how. I don't know if I can. I don't want you to leave," she said. I couldn't make sense of what she was saying.

"Delia, you know there is nothing you could say to get rid of me. Just tell me. Whatever it is, we'll fix it. Is it about the move? I told you, we'll make it work. You're dad's a prick, he won't be in D.C. forever. They'll vote him out soon enough." I was trying to make a joke, but she wasn't laughing. At all.

I moved closer to her and ran my finger up and down the length of her arm.

"Just tell me, please. You're really starting to freak me out," I said.

She finally looked up. Her eyes were already brimming with tears that were begging to spill over.

"Tobin, I'm pregnant," she said.

I lost my vision for a minute. Everything went completely blank. My sight, my thoughts. Everything.

"What? Are you sure?" We were always so careful. Always. I bet everyone says that when in this situation, but it's the truth.

"Of course I'm sure. I know how to count lines, Tobin. Two of them. Clear as day."

I ran my hand along my jaw, struggling to find the right words. Something to comfort her. Something to comfort myself. But I never found them. So in the end, I just backed off altogether. Stopped talking because I knew that nothing that I said would make it right.

- - -

I didn't know how to be what she needed from me then. I thought I was giving us both time to process it by avoiding her calls and giving her space. Or at least that's what I told myself. But she was right. I couldn't see what she needed from me through my own fear. My own selfishness.

It sounds stupid, but as close as D and I were, I never thought about kids before then. I honestly didn't know what I wanted. So in the end, I let her leave. I didn't even try to stop her. Knowing I may never see her again, knowing what she was going to have to go through on her own when she got to D.C. I bailed.

"I left you."

There I said it.

And then, because I don't know what else to do, and it's all I've wanted to do since the second she got to town, I tangle my fingers into the hair at the nape of her neck, pull her in close, inhale that sweet jasmine oil smell, and kiss her.

Her lips part with mine and she's actually kissing me back. I press harder into her. The need for her overwhelming want.

20
Delia

It used to be that there was no problem in the world that Tobin's kiss couldn't fix. My tears easily dried. The world quickly righted itself. But it feels so different now. So weighted. His lips so full of why's. How can I make him understand that things aren't that simple anymore?

"You can't do that, Tobin," I say, pulling away. "It's not fair." *Because I can't think when we touch that way,* and his kiss should NOT make me feel weak in the knees.

"Shit, Delia. I—"

"Totally wimped out when you knew I was pregnant. I could feel it in your voice. In your body. In the way you were suddenly needed for double shifts." We're still close. Too close for me think straight.

"But you—"

"Tobin, it was the scariest thing I'd ever done. I hated the decision. I hated knowing that I'd never see that baby's face. Never know what part of you and me would look like. But what was I supposed to do?

"Dad practically sent me away to have it done. It's not like I had any kind of plan. Like I had someone to raise a baby with, or someone to help me pick out parents to raise it. You weren't around! I lay in bed with cramps in a strange house for *days* second-guessing everything. You. Me. The baby. Everything. You should have been there."

Tobin's silent and staring. It's too much. It's *all* too much. The hurt still hovers between us, pushing and pulling on us like magnets.

"If you'd been with me, Tobin, fighting with me...I don't know."

"Did it ever occur to you that you should have stood up to him yourself? Make the people around you feel like they're worth it! Worth something!"

"Do you know how many times my dad was pissed at me over you? Have any idea how much pretending I've had to do to make up for it!"

"And was it worth it?" he spits out.

I ignore him. Because I have no idea what anything's worth any more.

"As soon as I felt good enough to get up and move around, Dad kept me busy. He sort of saved me that way. And—" And I can't believe I'm defending my father—especially to Tobin.

"Set you up with the perfect boyfriend."

"It took me *months* before I even held his hand! You hugged me in the driveway on the morning I left, and all I could feel was the distance you were putting between us, and the hurt of this huge decision we were supposed to make *together*! When you called, I realized that if you hated me, it would seal it. Us being apart. I let it happen that way. Because I knew if I felt like I couldn't have you, it might make it easier! But Weston and I weren't together then, Tobin. Not even close."

"Did it make it easier? Letting me hate you?" Something flashes across his face that I don't recognize. Remorse? Or maybe a new shade of anger.

"No! Yes!" I yell, and then I can feel my anger breaking down into something I don't want to feel at a bonfire with a group of friends. "I don't know!" Tears are falling freely down my cheeks.

"Delia." His voice breaks.

I take a step back, needing distance. "Yes. You know what? Yes. It helped knowing or hoping that you were more mad than hurt until I got here." And since then the anger's been killing me. Feeling like Tobin and I aren't over is killing me. Wanting to at least try again is killing me, and I didn't even totally realize it until now when we're standing here yelling at each other.

"Now what?"

"I don't know." I'm a mess. I need home, but not home. I don't want to face, Dad, Weston, Tobin…

Tobin reaches for me again, and I want it. I want him to touch me. I want to find a way to be around him, but I'm also too hurt to try anything right now.

"I gotta go."

And then I do. I spin away from the fire and our friends, get in Mom's car, and just drive away.

I drive around for more than an hour. Maybe two. I text Weston to tell him I'm safe. I don't dare talk to Mom or Dad. I may be eighteen. I may be graduated. But there's no mistaking I'm still in their mercy.

I can't believe that Tobin didn't see how obvious it was. How he was gone long before I was. Maybe he's starting to understand how it felt to be slowing losing him as my parents packed up our old life for our new.

"Let's just ease some of the pressure off both of us, Delia," Tobin said.

"What do you mean?" I asked my heart starting to pound. I only had three weeks left in town before our family moved.

"I mean it's hard on both of us with your dad breathing down our necks. Let's just lay low for a while and think. We'll figure it out." But the look in his eyes wasn't anything that resembled reassuring. It scared the hell out of me.

What else was I supposed to do but let him go? It was obvious that he didn't want the baby, the responsibility, *or* me. And right then, the tiniest part of me wondered if my dad hadn't been right about Tobin after all.

Even though I knew better. It was still Tobin who had pulled away first.

DESTINY

One for one?

Or a million for one?

Maybe two

Two lives

Two futures

Two choices

Just waiting

For a decision to be made

Like puzzle pieces

We fit

Filling holes

Making pictures

Making art

Making love

Or we don't.

21

Delia

I'm fairly sure that I've been crying for most of my drive, and when I stop in front of the house, I just sit in the car, wondering if I'm ready to go in.

My face is red, swollen, and my eyes are bloodshot. I'm a mess, but there's no prolonging the inevitable so I step out of the car, dreading what I'm about to do. I slide inside silently, and make my way to the living room where I hear voices.

"What happened?" Weston jumps up as I come into view.

Mom looks at me over her glass, with a raised eyebrow, and Dad follows Weston's lead and is now standing.

"Can I talk to you?" I ignore my father in favor of Weston, and lean my body toward the front door, hoping he'll follow.

He nods, takes my hand, and leads me outside, but there's something heavy between us that's never been there before.

I know what I have to do. Even though I don't get Tobin, don't even know if I can be *around* Tobin, Weston isn't it for me. It's horrible doing this to him, but he just isn't, and I've driven around and thought about it enough to know that I can't force him to be right for me. And I can't force myself to love him in the way that would make him right for me.

I lead him onto the front porch, and he closes the door quietly behind us. He's wary. I'm wary. I want to erase everything wrong with this situation, but I can't.

"Are you okay?" He steps toward me with his hand out, probably poised to pull me into him, to try to mend the sadness. But I don't think Weston's hands are capable of that anymore. Not in the way he'd want them to be.

"Weston, I—"

"Don't say it, Delia." He shakes his head, practically pleading with me.

"I'm going to." I have to.

"For him?" He lowers his head, but at least he doesn't say *him* the way I know Dad would.

I shake my head. "No. Not for him." Not even because of him, really. Because whether Tobin and I are together or not—and after today the chances are slim. "I just don't love you the way I should. It was okay when we were first dating, but it's not okay to keep being together. Not like this."

"So, it *is* because of him." Weston backs up a step, his eyes uncertain.

I close my eyes, wishing there was a way to make him understand. "One day you're going to meet a woman who sees everything wonderful about you and everything you hate about you, and make it all okay. And then you'll see why we didn't stay together."

He pulls in a few breaths and stares at the porch under our feet.

The silence is killing me. I'd rather him call me a whore and run away. Instead he steps closer and takes my hands in his. And now I'm crying again, because I do like this. Him. But I know it's not it. And it's not even that I'm looking for someone to be married to, it's that I know I will never marry Weston, and he wants to move that way. It isn't fair.

"I already did, Delia."

My chest drops.

He pulls me close enough to kiss my cheek, and then without another word he spins around and heads inside.

I hate him a little for not fighting with me. *For* me. But the same thing also brings relief.

I slump against the side of the house. I'm just a destroyer I guess. A selfish destroyer. I don't mean to be. I definitely don't *want* to be. How could Weston feel that way about me? I've felt close to him, but not *that* close. Maybe it's just that what we had was the closest he'd ever been to someone.

I want to be as strong as the wall I'm leaning against. Actually, I'd go for anyone stronger than me right now. But I did just let Weston go—one part of my safety-net. What else do I need to do? And how many people will I hurt or make angry to get me what I want? No. What I need.

Needing out of my dress, I decide to brave inside.

"Delia!" Dad yells. "Where have you been? We had *reservations*! You are not to blow off your family like that."

"Dad." My voice is soft. I don't have anything else in me right now. "One of my close friends was buried today."

I stare at him and plead for him to understand. But I can see that he doesn't.

"We went to dinner without you. Weston had to cover for you." His brows come up, and his lurking form sends my insides shaking.

I ignore him. And just before I start for upstairs, Weston's walking down. With his suitcase.

"What's going on, son?" Dad asks. His tone in addressing Weston is all kind politeness. Or maybe it's just politic settling in.

Weston glances briefly my direction before resting his eyes on Dad. "I have that thing in Baton Rouge tomorrow with my dad, and Tennessee a few days after, so…"

Dad's jaw tightens as his eyes go between us. "Guess I'll see you there."

"I'll walk you out." I turn to the door.

Neither Weston nor Dad says anything. Walking through the room is like moving through syrup. Weston opens the door for me like always, and I step into the pools of light in the driveway.

I feel Dad watching us as the door closes behind Weston who steps around me and almost breaks into a run getting to his car.

"Weston?"

"Don't." Weston turns to face me before jerking open the back door of his car, throwing his suitcase inside and slamming it shut.

I don't think I've ever seen Weston feel so much— or maybe it's that I've never seen him *show* what he feels so much.

"I'm sorry, I—" I almost step toward him, but to do what?

Weston keeps his voice quiet. "Don't give me any bullshit line about it not being about him, Delia. I'm not stupid. A few days ago when you left town, you clutched onto me like your life depended on it. About like you held him today. Right in front of me. Don't feed me anymore bullshit and I'll keep my mouth shut about what happened between us."

Before I can make a snide remark about life not being about a series of appearances, he's slammed the door and pulled out. Maybe I do want the nice guy he was on the porch.

I just need more space. Somewhere I can breathe.

"Delia. What the hell is going on?" Dad's voice booms out behind me.

"He told you, Daddy." I turn and put on my best sweet smile. "He had to go."

In a move I don't think I've ever done before, I push my way around Dad and head for the stairs. Instead of making everything better, I've made it all worse.

Tobin and I are in a fight—or a continuation of the year-old fight. Though, it all had to come out at some point if we're going to see each other. Weston's pissed at me, and Dad's anger is brewing downstairs. If he doesn't have it out with me tonight, tomorrow's really going to suck.

I suddenly feel this urgency to fix it. *All of it.* I can't be with Weston, but that doesn't mean he shouldn't know how he helped me, how important he was. How he was my friend when I needed one, and my support in the whole new world Dad dragged me into.

And I'll also need to talk to Dad, but I don't even know how to start that, yet.

But Tobin. That's something I might be able to fix. Or maybe it's just the thing I'm most desperate to fix. We might not be together, but I can't take it if we're not friends. I can't be okay if Tobin isn't in my life *somehow*.

I loved him so much. Love him. There's no way I can tell myself it's not still there—it's just that there's this huge mess in the way. Like all the power behind how I felt for him changed when he hurt me, made me mad, and now, being around him again, it's changing back.

A shiver runs through me as I think about the night at the cabin. THE night at the cabin. The first of many. The first where we... My cheeks heat up at the thought of it. Of him.

∽

I stood backwards on the ladder and he came up a step so our feet were on the same rung, still underwater. He looked down at me with his deep brown eyes, making my heart beat like crazy.

"A kiss for a kiss?" he asked like always.

I clutched the ladder with all my strength, leaned forward and touched our lips together. He let me move away before leaning in to give me the same soft kiss I'd just given him. Something was different. Something I couldn't put my finger on.

"Another kiss for a kiss?" I asked, already feeling out of breath. The heat from his body kept me warm as the breeze drifted across the lake.

He leaned in first this time, and parted his lips just slightly, just enough that I wanted to kiss him harder, deeper. To taste the beer and lake water and whatever else made Tobin taste like Tobin. When I kissed him back, I wasn't as careful.

There was no kiss for a kiss. I couldn't back myself away from him if I'd wanted to.

By the time we did break away, I was out of breath, and he'd nearly fallen off the ladder.

"You are one dangerous girl, Delia Gentry." He grabbed me by the waist and hoisted me onto the dock.

I realized as my bum hit the boards, once again in just my bra and panties that I trusted Tobin. I trusted his eyes, and I trusted his kiss.

"Wanna go inside?" he asked.

Something was definitely different. The air between us tense and intense and charged with a million things I wanted to feel around Tobin forever.

I stood up on the dock. He gathered our things, and carried them toward the door of the small cabin. This cabin that had been abandoned long ago by strangers that we'd claimed as ours.

The moment we stepped inside I forced myself to speak. "My wet clothes for yours?"

I swear I heard the air leave his lungs as he turned to face me. "You sure?"

"You chicken?"

He dropped our dry clothes on the floor and carefully pulled me toward him. I pushed down on his boxers, and he unsnapped my bra, and then after a few really deep breaths, I pulled off my panties while he watched, jaw slack, and I laid down on the bed, pretending to be way braver than I felt.

He scrambled out of his soaked boxers, and crawled onto the mattress. His body was on me, the weight of him warming me in a way I'd never experienced before, and it was like he already couldn't catch his breath. Or maybe that was me. Both of us probably.

He was propped on his elbows, keeping most of his weight off of me. "Are you scared?"

"No," I lied.

"Well I am." His eyes never wavered from mine. "I promise, I'll—"

I cut him off with my lips. I know he was worried about being my first. He had told me so. There were so many times he had put off us being together no mater how badly I could tell he wanted me.

I loved him. I trusted him. And I wanted him.

- - -

As much as part of me wants to slide out the window, drop and run, I slide in to my blankets and just wish for a good night's sleep. Actually, if I'm making wishes, I wish to wake up in the morning knowing exactly what I need to do, but I can't imagine that'll happen. Instead I wonder if Tobin's finding any amount of peace tonight.

22
Tobin

"Thanks for everything, man," I say to Nelson. I pick up a pile of empty cups and toss them into a garbage bag.

"Hey, that's nothing, Tobin. We miss Eamon, too," he says.

"Tobin, please call us if you need something, we love you," Leslie says. She stands on her tip toes to kiss my cheek.

"Yes, Ma'am."

"You thinking about her?" Leslie asks.

"Thinking about who?" I ask. The girl I've never been able to erase from my thoughts? That one?

"Oh please, I saw the way you guys looked at each other earlier."

"She was just helping me with some ice. Don't make it into something its not. Besides, I don't have feelings for her anymore." I shake my head and stuff a few more cups into the garbage bag.

She shakes her head.

"Tobin, you were in love with that girl," Leslie says. "You haven't just forgotten all of that. You should see her again. It might do you some good to get a little closure."

I stare up at the sky. Waiting for all of the answers to fall from it is futile, but right now, it's all I've got. I don't have any idea what to do about anything.

"Yeah, well, it's easy to throw out advice when it's someone else's life," I say.

She gives me a small nod and a quick smile that says she's going to drop it.

"Hey, are you going to be okay to drive home?" Leslie asks.

"I'm good. I haven't had anything to drink tonight, but I'm staying here at the cabin anyway." I point to the small abandoned cabin behind us. It's no bigger than my bedroom at home, but it was the perfect size to spend a night alone...or with someone you loved. I still hadn't decided if it was stupid not to have chased after Delia earlier. God, I'd missed the feeling of her mouth on mine. I shake my head to clear the memory and say the rest of my goodbyes. But it's not that easy. This place is full of memories of her.

I flung her onto the makeshift bed and inched up the length of her body. Taking my time, touching every inch of skin, kissing every flawless curve.

There were so many nights that we spent here

together. But that first one, I didn't see that one coming.

I'd never been scared to be with a woman before, but Delia, the thought of being with her, well, I was nervous. Nervous I'd hurt her. That it wouldn't live up to whatever she had in her head. Nervous that she'd freak out afterward. Nervous that I'd fuck it all up.

I'd never been with someone that I loved before. Shit, I'd never even been a girl's first. It was moments like that, that made Delia's father's words ring true. There was no way that I was good enough for her. I didn't deserve to be touching her. Loving her. It didn't help that that night we'd gotten into our first and only real fight. It was the night of that damn fundraiser. Such a ridiculous affair it seemed fit for a movie, not real life.

The Crawford Country Club was never my scene, but especially not on that night, when the place was packed full of deep pocketed politicians and their supporters, who all couldn't wait to get in line to kiss Delia's father's ass and make him the next Louisiana Senator. I'd be lying if I said I didn't swipe a couple of flutes of champagne when no one was looking. I needed something to calm my nerves in this place. Why had I let Delia talk me into this? Sure she did things with me and my family, but we weren't like the Gentry's.

We all hung out on the river, barbequed, drank beer and got too loud. We didn't put on a big show like this. I was already on edge and out of place when Mr. Gentry started walking toward us.

"Tobin, so nice of you to accompany Delia tonight," he said.

I smiled a thin, tight smile, knowing that he was completely full of shit. He couldn't stand me.

"Delia, you look beautiful as always," he said. "Tobin, son, I assume you won't mind me borrowing my daughter for a moment. I've got someone I want to introduce her to."

I nodded as he led her away from me. Did I mind? If I did, it wouldn't matter. I never had a choice when it came to her dear old dad. It did give me the opportunity to grab another glass of liquid courage, though.

Across the room, I watched Mr. Gentry introduce Delia to a guy. He looked about my age. Delia tugged on her bangs, looking flustered and uncomfortable.

She glanced over her shoulder at me. "Sorry," she mouthed.

All I could do was shrug. I wasn't stupid. I knew exactly what her father was doing. Trying to find a replacement for me. Trying to find someone suitable. Someone worthy of his precious daughter.

The discomfort I felt quickly grew into anger when her father walked off, leaving Delia with the stranger. I watched them laugh together. He touched her elbow and my skin prickled with irritation. She didn't shrug away from his touch, and I think that's what made me the most upset. Sure he wanted to touch her. I bet every man in this room wanted to. The point was she shouldn't have been so comfortable with it. Or maybe that was just the bubbly talking.

"Sorry about that, you know my dad, he just can't help himself," She tried to link her arm through mine when she came back a few minutes later, but I shrugged it off.

"May be an inherited trait."

She pulled her brows together in confusion.

"What's that supposed to mean?" she asked.

I sighed. "Nothing, you just didn't look too bothered by him."

"Oh Tobin, you're being ridiculous."

I felt then like I was so childish. Such a bother to her.

"Maybe that's all I am. Maybe that's all *we* are. Just ridiculous," I said.

"You really want to do this? You're just letting my father win if you do." Her lips pressed tightly together. Delia might not agree with her father, but she was an expert at playing his games. She knew how to put on a smile for show and if I was going to be with her, I knew that I was going to have to learn to do the same.

She reached over and grasped my hand. I leaned down and kissed her on top of her head.

"So, about that swim later," I said with a smile.

"Funny thing about that," she whispered. "I didn't bring a swimsuit."

"That's never been a problem before," I said. "Tell you what, you don't wear yours, I won't wear mine."

"You're making some tough deals tonight, Mr. LeJeune. I think these guys might be rubbing off on you." She laughed and stood on her tiptoes to kiss me.

- - -

The fire is dwindling, so I kick some sand into it and watch the flames slowly disappear. Unable to breathe. Choking. Like I've felt the last few days. I close my eyes and I'm back at the Country Club.

⟶

"So, do you have plans after this? I thought maybe we could go find something to do together?" The strange guy said. I had gone to get our coats and neither Delia, nor the tuxedo-wearing-jackass knew I'd come back and was standing right behind them.

"No, sorry. I've got plans. And um, also, I'm seeing someone," Delia said.

"Seeing someone, or *seriously* seeing someone?" He laughed. He thought he was so clever. I worked my jaw back and forth, my anger rising by the second.

"It's pretty serious." Delia let out a soft laugh. You could tell that she was uncomfortable but didn't want to be rude.

"That's not what your dad said." He reached out and touched her waist. The way that I would. The way that no one else should.

Delia raised an eyebrow, looking equal parts annoyed and surprised.

That was it. I rounded the large row of potted plants and clutched her hand.

"Tobin, hey," Delia said.

"I've got your coat. Let's go." I admit, my tone was harsh when I grabbed her hand and tried to pull her away. I probably looked like the asshole jealous boyfriend, and I sort of was right then.

"Okay, sure." She nodded. "It was nice meeting you... What did you say your name was again?" I was ticked off at her politeness. I just wanted to leave already.

"Russell. Russell Gautreaux," he said. He flashed an arrogant smile directed at me when he said, "And Delia, let me know if you ever change your mind."

I didn't even think about it. I just reacted. With jealousy. And anger. And annoyance at Delia's father, and at her unwavering manners. It only took an instant for my fist to connect with his jaw, and for Russell Gautreaux to be laid out on the ballroom floor. He rubbed his chin and blinked over and over again, like he was in shock.

"Tobin, what the hell?" Delia whispered loudly. She smacked me on the arm with her small clutch of a purse and then started dragging me to the exit.

A ring of people had already gathered around Russell. The older women shook their heads at me like I was a pariah as we made our way out the doors.

"He shouldn't have acted like that. He shouldn't have put his hands on you," I said. I unlocked the passenger door to my truck for her and held it open.

"I'm not getting in there until you apologize."

I laughed. "Apologize for what?"

"Tobin, I don't need you to look out for me. I don't need you to protect me—"

"Well too bad. I'm going to do those things whether you like it or not, Delia."

"And I certainly don't need you beating someone up for me. I can't believe you did this. *Here.* Those people paid two grand a plate and you caused the biggest scene ever. They will never stop talking about this!"

She was shivering. I was still holding her coat.

"I'm not going to apologize for hitting that creep, D." I draped the long black coat over her shoulders.

"Of course you're not. You don't even see what you did. You're just begging my father to hate you even more by doing things like that. Is that what you want?"

I stood there staring at her. What the fuck did she want me to say? The guy had it coming. Any normal person would've done the same thing.

"You know Tobin, I've stood in between you and my dad for months now," she said.

"I never asked you to do that."

"Yeah, and I never asked you to go ape shit on some guy at my father's party!" She so rarely swore that I couldn't help but smile. "The point is, no matter what my dad has ever said about you, how you aren't good enough, or this—this trying to set me up with someone else—I've never," she said. She stopped and stared down at her hands.

"Just say it, Delia."

"I've never been embarrassed to be with you until tonight. I can't believe you did this."

She turned and started to walk away.

"D, I'm sorry!" I apologized.

Too late.

She was gone.

I thought she was done with me for good. That

was the first time I'd ever apologized for something that I wasn't truly sorry for to anyone but my mama—and then, it was only because I was going to get the belt if I didn't.

I drove out to the lake because I was too riled up to go home. I didn't want to have to explain to Eamon what had happened. I knew he'd say he told me so. And he did. Repeatedly.

"An olive branch for an olive branch?" she asked. I didn't hear her coming. She was barefoot, holding her black shoes in one hand.

"Jesus, I'm sorry, Delia." I jumped up and pulled her into my arms.

"How's the hand?" she asked.

I shrugged.

"I didn't mean what I said earlier, I promise," she said.

I caught her chin between my thumb and index finger and kissed the tip of her nose. "I wouldn't blame you if you did."

"I just—"

"You don't have to explain," I said.

"No, I want to. I just feel like to my dad, my mom and I are possessions. He controls us, he treats us like we are things that he owns, not people. And I love that I've never felt like you did that with me. Until tonight. I'm sorry, I know I overreacted. And that guy was a total jerk—"

I kissed her. Our mouths pressed hard together like everything that we needed to say was being communicated that way. And it was all good and right.

"Slow down. I still owe you a swim," she said, tugging her zipper down and sliding her dress to the ground.

I chased her into the water with my clothes still on and we swam and kissed and touched.

She was both the most innocent and most dangerous girl I had ever met. I loved that she stuck up to me. I loved that I ached when she left me standing there, that I actually cared enough to hurt. I'd never felt that with any girl before her. And that night at the cabin, we made love for the first time.

- - -

I haven't stayed at the cabin in about a year, but nothing has changed. The tiny cabinet full of random supplies—garbage bags, batteries, condoms, is still untouched, and my sleeping bag is still neatly rolled up in the corner. I spread it out on the thin cot mattress and lay down. The heavy weight of the day settles into my bones and I know that I could easily fall asleep for days. When I close my eyes, though, my mind shifts back to all the nights we spent here.

I came here after Delia and I said good-bye the last night because I knew it'd still smell like her. Her hairpins would still be on the windowsill where she took them out and left them. Her copy of Whitman's *Leaves of Grass* would still be lying next to the makeshift bed, with the last page she read dog-eared. I sort of wish I would have left it here now to thumb through.

Back then, reminders of Delia were too hard to have around. It was like the entire place reeked of regret. But I don't think I feel that way anymore. I got too close, fell too hard, and let her in too much. I broke every one of the LeJeune brother's rules when I was with Delia. But I broke every single one of them for her.

Eamon tried to help me forget her and move on by keeping me busy. He and I built homemade land mines and threw rocks at them to watch them explode, glass flying through the air. We went jumping off the highest rocks into water that was way too shallow. Eamon said that he did all of those things to make himself feel alive. He saved me then and a lot of times since. I don't think there will ever be a time that I won't miss my brother.

23

Delia

You'd think after the last few days, the cemetery is the last place I'd want to be, but I miss Gram. Dad's gone to meet up with Weston and his father, and I definitely can't lie around with Mom and think about how bad that meeting might be going.

I park at the bottom of the hill and start the short walk up. I should have worn different shoes; the heels of my sandals sink into the damp soil with each step. They'll probably be ruined after this little field trip. No, what I *really* should have done was bring flowers. Magnolias were grandma's favorite. I reach into my pocket and make sure that I remembered to put a couple of Kleenex. I'm alone, but I know after talking to Gram, I'll end up crying. When I look back up, I realize that there is someone already standing at Gram's grave.

Tobin? What in the world? I walk slowly to where he stands. I don't want to interrupt him, but I also don't want to startle him.

I stand next to him without saying a word. He knows I'm here. I can tell because he gives a small nod. There are two Magnolias on her headstone. He must have brought them from the tree on his property. I don't know what to say. So I just stare. My heart pounding. My throat drying out.

We went from yelling to this.

Out of the corner of my eye, I see him do the sign of the cross and then hear him clear his throat, so I figure it's safe to speak.

"What are you doing here?" I ask. I don't look away from the spot on Gram's grave that I've been staring at for the last few minutes and neither does he. We just stand there, side by side, my shoulder almost touching his chest.

"Sorry, I didn't know you'd be here." His voice is gravely and hoarse. Has he been crying?

"Same," I say. "You brought flowers?"

I see him nod again. I hate that this is awkward.

"The Magnolia tree on our land had just bloomed. I know they were her favorite."

My heart swells that he remembered that about Gram. She would be horrified at what had become of Tobin and I. She always had such a soft spot for him, and faith in us as a couple.

"That was really nice of you. Thank you." I'm pathetic. This is… There aren't words for how incredible this is. It's so easy to remember all the crazy stuff and all the passion stuff, but it's this boy, this man that I loved. Love.

"Look, I just came to bring the flowers and clean up around the stone. I'll get out of your way now."

"Wait," I say. "Do you, like, do that often?" My heart still pounds. And we're not yelling. Last time I saw him we were yelling. Too many things whirl through my head and my heart right now for me to say anything I need to say.

"Who else is going to do it, Delia? Your grandmother was always really kind to me, it's the least I can do for her."

"Well, I appreciate it. And you don't have to go. I mean, I don't mind if you stay while I'm here."

He finally turns to look at me and all of the air leaves my body when I see the broken look on his face.

"Can I say something, D?" When he calls me D, like old times, goose bumps cover my arms.

It's my turn to nod.

"I'm sorry for being a jerk about you coming to town. I don't blame you for moving on. I don't blame you for hating me—"

"I don't hate you, Tobin," I clarify.

I can't tell for sure, but he looks visibly relieved by that statement.

"I know that I didn't support you the way that you needed. That I wasn't there for you. Part of me felt like I wanted to have this family with you, but the other part just wanted to run away. I just, I feel like I screwed everything up—"

"Tobin, we were in it together. It wasn't just you that was confused. I was a little out of my mind, too." I can't believe we're doing this with the way we lashed out at each other last night. My chest aches at being so close to him, at starting to wish for something that we might not ever get to have. I miss being with Tobin.

My feet continue to sink into the wet ground. It's obvious that neither one of us has any idea what to say. How to heal any of the hurt between us. So we just stand there for another eternity in silence before I speak again.

"Do you remember that time we went to New Orleans? When I got you those tickets to see The Molly Ringwalds?" I ask.

"How could I forget? I almost ended up in jail." The corner of his mouth pulls up and something almost like a smile is on Tobin's face.

"You did not." I scoff.

"Delia, when that drunken frat boy on Bourbon grabbed you, I lost my mind." His eyes widen as bit as he speaks, remembering that crazy weekend.

It's partially true. Some random drunken jackass grabbed me and stuck his tongue down my throat. When I tried to pull away, he wouldn't let go, and when he leaned in for another kiss, I smacked him, right across his already red cheeks. He threw me onto the filthy, pot-hole covered ground, along with the ice cold hurricane he was drinking.

I'd never seen anyone as mad as Tobin that night.

He didn't hesitate. His fist connected with frat-boy's jaw so hard that he flew backward. Tobin jumped on top of him and continued to punch him over and over and over again. There was blood pouring from every bit of frat-boy's face, his nose was obviously broken, and yet Tobin continued.

I didn't recognize the Tobin that I saw that night— bruised fists, shirt covered in blood splatters. It took Eamon and two other strangers to pull Tobin off of the guy, and by that time, his friends had already gone to find the police.

When the two cops showed up, Eamon took the blame. Even though he stood there in a perfectly clean shirt without a scratch on him, he didn't waver.

"You never would have gone to jail. Eamon never would have let that happen," I say.

"Well, we're lucky the guy was too embarrassed to give a statement. What's your point?" he asks.

"The kind of bond you two had was incredible."

"*Had*, being the operative word."

My hand twitches as I think about touching him. Reaching out and letting my hand slide down his arm. "He's here with you, Tobin. Just like Gram is still with me. And I know that you believe that, or you wouldn't be standing here now."

He doesn't say anything.

"He came to see me, Tobin. Before I left. Before the baby was…gone." I was so surprised to see Eamon. No announcement, nothing. Just showed up.

He reaches up and pinches the bridge of his nose and shakes his head. "Did he upset you?"

"No, nothing like that. He came to let me know that he was behind us, no matter what we decided to do. He said he'd do anything to help us either way. He told me that he had some money saved, that he was making more than enough out at the plants. He had enough for a down payment on a house set aside, but he would give it to me if you and I decided to keep the baby. That we could use it to have a fresh start, to move away from here, away from my dad…

"I told him I couldn't take money that he was planning to use for a home for himself. He joked and said he didn't need a house of his own anyway. He said that if he had one, he wouldn't have any good excuses to give the girls who always want to stay the night with him." I laugh remembering how I chuckled through my never ending tears when Eamon told me that.

"Why didn't you ever tell me?" Tobin asks.

The pads of our fingers lightly graze together. I want with everything in me to reach over and hold his hand, but I can't.

"Tobin, I tried. You barely returned my calls. When you did, we'd sit in silence. I didn't know how to bring it up, or if I even should. And honestly, part of me felt like I couldn't. I didn't want to influence your decision either way. And I didn't want to take you away from your brother. I was scared about the baby. I was scared that no matter what we did, you'd end up resenting me."

He swallows again and again. Like he's trying to digest my words.

"Delia, I don't know what to say."

"I know. There really isn't anything to say."

The silence is back. The words are all spoken. The only thing left to do is walk away. Again. The anger and hurt in Tobin's face when he yelled at me was real. I'm not sure if it's something he'll ever be able to let go of, but at least we're talking without yelling. Forgiving someone is a scary thing, because you have to trust that you won't be hurt again, and I hope we're there. Or will be soon.

"Good-bye, Tobin," I say.

I close the space between us and stand on my tip-toes. I kiss his cheek lightly and then turn and leave. I can't do Gram and Tobin in one day. My heart can't take it.

By the time I make it home, Mom's passed out on the sofa, and Dad's nowhere to be found. Guess he won't be back 'til tomorrow. No Mom. No Dad. No Weston. I wander through the silent house. The whole time I was growing up this house was silent or so tense that the air felt hard to breathe.

I'm suddenly not sure how I survived it, but I do know I'm going to ask to spend some time here. Alone. I can't even think about what Dad's going to say. Not yet. It makes me feel weak that I'm afraid even to ask. I laughed when Carl at the bar said I was graduated—somehow implying that I could do what I wanted.

The only time I've done exactly what I wanted is when I was doing exactly what Dad didn't want me to do. I sit on a stool in the dark kitchen. The house still in silence.

I want out. I just got back, and I want out.

Maybe I'll finally take a trip to the lake and spend some time. I should be tired, but I'm not, so I grab an apple from the fridge and walk out of the house.

"Delia!" Kelly waves from her truck parked in my driveway.

"Hey." I walk her direction, having no idea why they're here.

"Hey, Delia. Jump on in." Rachel scoots to the middle seat.

"What are you doing here?" I ask.

Kelly laughs. "Lookin' for you crazy girl."

I slide in without thinking. "Where y'all headed?"

"Since we're both sober, we have no idea," Kelly teases.

"I was headed to the lake. Do you think you could

drop me off at the tracks?" I ask. Walking to the lake from the crossing would be a lot easier than navigating my overgrown trail.

Rachel's brow comes up and this sneaky, knowing, smile. "Hoping to run into anybody?"

"Whose name rhymes with Row-bin?" Kelly laughs as she hits the gas, lurching her beast of a truck forward.

My cheeks heat up. "I don't know. I just…"

Rachel bumps my shoulder. "You don't have to say nothin' Delia. Even if you didn't run into him, probably a lot of good memories there."

"You guys talkin' without yellin'?" Kelly asks.

"Did you know he's been takin' care of Gram's gravesite?" I lean forward to catch their expressions.

"Nope." Kelly shakes her head. "But that sounds like a Tobin thing."

I slump in my seat. It *is* a Tobin thing. Eamon may have taken care of Tobin, but Tobin did his fair share of taking care of his brother, too. Tobin spent a lot of time taking care of me—even things I probably should have been able to do on my own.

"You stickin' around for a while?" Rachel's voice is thick with something she thinks she knows.

"I'm stayin' for me. No one else."

Kelly lets out a whoop from the driver's seat. "For real? You're gonna be here a while?"

"Yeah." I nod. Now I'm definitely feeling more confident.

"Told ya they'd get back together," Rachel says.

"Oh." I shake my head. "We're not yellin' anymore, but…"

Kelly lets out a scoff. "He has not even smiled at another girl since you left, Delia. That boy is still full-on, hung up, in love, with you."

She pulls to a stop at the crossing, and I'm out of breath.

Is Tobin still in love with me? Talking about forgiveness when I wasn't sure what was left of us is one thing. Thinking about the kind of forgiveness that would help Tobin and I more forward is something else.

"Want company?" Rachel asks.

"Nah. Not tonight." I jump out of the truck next to the tracks.

"Should we tell Tobin you're lookin' for him if we run into him?" Rachel leans out of the window.

I think for a minute before answering. "Yeah. Tell him I'm lookin' for him."

"You got it, girl." Kelly honks once before they back up, turn around, and drive out of sight.

And I guess it's that simple. I'm looking for Tobin.

24

Tobin

I flop back on the mattress in the cabin. I'm sure I should be home, but after spending one night in this place, and then seeing Delia today, I just...ended up back here. I miss her so much. Eamon's death is a gaping hole, but to have Delia so close is like torture. At least the... *Weston* wasn't with her today.

"Is there room for one more?" Delia's voice cuts through the silence. And for a moment, I really think my heart may have stopped beating.

How could I have not realized it before now? Standing right in front of me, warm, breathing, gorgeous, was all that I ever needed to make *me* feel alive.

"...." My mouth is agape, but no words will come out.

"Sorry, I didn't mean to sneak up on you. I just—I just couldn't leave things the way they were, Tobin."

She drops her hand from the doorframe and takes the few steps toward the small bed.

"You can sit," I say.

She nods and takes a seat cross-legged across from me. Her knee touches my leg, just like we always sit like this. Just like we haven't yelled at each other, and just like we haven't avoided each other for a year.

"Is that my shirt?" I can't help but smile as I finger the soft fabric. She must've taken it before she left.

She shrugs with a hint of a smile. "I'm a thief. What can I say?"

"I didn't expect to see you again," I admit. When she told me goodbye at the cemetery, I figured that was her last stop before taking off.

"Yeah, I really don't know what I'm doing here. All the times we've talked in the last few days, and I just feel like there is still so much we haven't said..." Her voice trails off. There's a rogue piece of hair that has fallen out of her ponytail. I reach over and tuck it behind her ear and she leans into my hand. It's all too damn confusing. I don't understand how she can want to be here with me, and how desperately I want her here and we can still have all of this misunderstanding between us.

"Delia, can I ask you something?"

She nods, looking a little worried.

I take a deep breath, because we've never really talked about it.

"Tobin, what are we going to do?" she asked me for the millionth time that afternoon. We were sitting on my porch, the air was too thick and sticky to form a coherent thought, at least that's what I'd like to blame it on.

"It's not my decision, D. Whatever you think is best. It's your body. I'll go along with whatever," I said.

She stared up at me, her eyes pleading. Back then I couldn't understand what the pleading was for. Now I know it was resolve. She wanted me to have the answers, or to at least man-up and pretend that I did. But Delia and I were both weak in different ways.

"I just don't know what to do. My dad doesn't want me to keep it. He says I'm not ready. I know I'm not, but it's not just me, Tobin. This baby is ours. It's part of both of us."

It felt like she wanted me to make the decision for her, but I couldn't. No matter what I told her to do, it'd be the wrong. Either way, she would end up hating me for telling her what to do.

"He says that we should take care of it when we get to D.C.," she said.

"Why there? I can't leave work. I can't be with you then," I told her. Making it about me, of course. And part of it probably was. If I couldn't be there, her dad had even more control. We'd had such a hard time even talking to each other then, I wasn't sure what to say.

"He says there'd be no way to keep it quiet if I did it here. Or even in Baton Rouge, someone would find out." She pulled her knees up to her chest and buried her face into her hands. I pulled her in close to me, but it didn't feel like it used to. Touching her used to be second nature and now it felt mechanical. Like I was following some sort of manual.

I didn't know how to be the person I used to be with her when I was causing her so much pain.

- - -

"Do you regret the choice we made?" I ask.

She picks at some fuzz on the old blanket for a moment and then finally looks up.

"That's the thing, Tobin. It was never *our* decision. Whether it's the one that you ultimately wanted me to make or not, you never made that known. You let me take responsibility for all of it. I'm the one who had to own what I did. Just me," she says.

"And that's why you're so angry at me?" I let my gaze drop this time. I can't even look at her. She's absolutely right about everything. I vividly remember every single time I promised her I'd never leave her. I'd always take care of things. I didn't lie, but I definitely failed.

"You already asked me that, Tobin. I'm not angry. I was never *angry.*" She pauses. "Okay. I might have been angry for a while." The corner of her mouth pulls up in a half-smile.

I wonder if she's thinking about the slough of cussing she gave me over the phone.

"I needed time to process everything. Just like you did. But I had to make the decision before I was allowed that time. But no, to answer your question, I don't regret it. Neither one of us were equipped to deal with a situation that big at that moment. I don't regret what we did, but the guilt of it keeps me up at night sometimes. And afterward, talking to you only reminded me of the choice," she says. "And my dad…it was too much for me to deal with on my own."

It all starts coming into place now. Lone puzzle pieces finally linking up. So much miscommunication. So much unspoken hurt.

"So, where does that leave us now?" I ask boldly.

She shrugs.

"Somewhere on the outside of hurt. On the outside of loss. Somewhere complicated. Somewhere…hopeful," she says.

There's a long pause. I pull her into me, and the warmth of her makes me tremble. "Stay."

"I don't want to fight with you anymore. I don't want you to hate me anymore. Even now, no one in my life knows me like you do."

It shouldn't come out, but it does anyway. "Even Weston?"

25

Delia

"Couldn't help yourself, could you?" I try to put enough tease in my voice that he knows its okay. Lord knows I'd have a million questions to ask him if he'd been seeing someone else.

"Sorry. You don't have to answer, Delia."

"Weston was a friend when I needed one, but he would have been shocked and appalled at the girl who leaned as far over the counter as she could to coax a beer out of Carl. We never…" I hope I don't have to say it, but my cheeks are heating up, and Tobin can read me.

Tobin chuckles, and his arms squeeze me closer to him. It's like there were these walls between Tobin and I, and the more we talk and the more we lie together, the more they fade. The closer we get to getting a chance to see what we could have had together without the mess.

"You know what scares me?" I ask. Now that I feel like we actually might make this work. Might pull this together.

"Hmm." His hand doesn't stop touching me. Running up and down my arm, on my side, in my hair.

"That all the hurt we share will take too long to go away." I don't know if Tobin will even understand what I mean.

He's silent, but hasn't stopped touching me. This means he's thinking.

"Do you know what I'm talking about?"

"I know what you're talking about." His fingers touch the back of my neck and I know he wants me to look at him.

I roll onto my side, putting us so close, but still not close enough. "Tobin." I let my hand rest against his cheek.

"You're everything, Delia. And all that history, it's just going to make us stronger, you know?"

I close my eyes and realize that I might get to have this. Him. Tobin. Any part of him is better than none of him. To salvage anything of the mess we made would be a miracle. "I want it to."

"So do I. And I think that's enough." He studies me for a moment, his body tenses. "Do you?"

"Yes. Yes, I do." I lie back down and bury my face in the side of his neck to breathe him in. His whole body loosens and relaxes, then pulls us together.

The first night I spent the night in this little place with Tobin I was so worried that I'd fall asleep, and wouldn't make it home before Mom and Dad woke up. I'm not going to worry about that tonight because I'm done caring what Dad thinks about Tobin.

"Delia?" Tobin shifts on the small bed and I turn to face him, very aware that we're stomach to stomach, chest to chest, and hip to hip.

"Yes?" I answer, my breath already half-stolen from me.

He touches my chin, just like he always used to—between index finger and thumb. "I'm so sorry. About everything. I'm sorry I let my fear getting in the way of talking to you before you left and I'm sorry I didn't try harder to keep us together."

The sorrow is heavy in his eyes and on the corners of his mouth, which are turned down.

I set my hand on his. "I'm sorry, too. About everything."

His brow comes down as he moves toward me, and then hesitates. Everything inside me feels loose and shaky with anticipation, like I'm about to fall apart and need Tobin to hold me together.

Instead of pressing our lips together, I bury my face in his chest, almost afraid of what I'll feel. Will there be more hurt? Will his kiss hit me the way it always did and make me lose my head? I'm not sure I can handle either right now.

"Delia." His fingers slide through my hair.

"Hmmm?" I smile as relief starts to fill me, take me over. If I thought I was lighter when I sent out that email

and a text, it's nothing compared to how I feel now. I lean off his chest to see his face.

"I can't give you the life that you're used to." His eyes look down and won't meet mine.

"Thank God." I laugh. It's a real one, and feels amazing.

Tobin's smile is everything as he wraps his arms more tightly around me, and right now, just being here is enough.

Hours later, I'm still drifting in and out of sleep, but Tobin's out. My week's been nothing like his. It'll probably be a long time before the loss of Eamon loosens its hold, but I plan to be here for it.

As much as I want to lie with Tobin until he wakes up, and then watch his smile spread as he sees me, there are a few things that I need to do first. I scan the cabinet for a pencil, paper, or anything, but I don't see what I need. I stand and watch him sleep knowing that I'm as much in love with him as ever. Knowing that what we had was a lot more than a teenage crush, and knowing I'm going to do whatever it takes for us to be together again.

The walk home is quiet. Peaceful. I've hardly slept in days, but just those few hours under Tobin's arm…it was enough. Just enough to give me the strength to do what I need to. I'm not leaving Crawford again, at least not unless it's on my own terms. And as much as I'd love to lean on Tobin for all of this, I know part of my problem is that I've let too many different people at too many different times carry me, lead me, and help me.

Knowing that Tobin will be around at the end of this is enough.

I shuffle along the tracks, dread starting to sink in at what I'm about to do. I always joke to myself about my dad being a crazy asshole, but I wonder how much it would take to actually send him over the edge.

I didn't have morning sickness, I got sick at night. Having my own bathroom helped, but not enough. One week in, hardly a word from Tobin, and I was once again hunched over the toilet.

Mom stopped, looked me up and down once, and she knew. She just knew.

"Mom..." I wanted to explain, but there was nothing to explain. I was pregnant, and Dad was going to be furious.

"Stay here, Delia."

I jumped to follow her, knowing she was going to tell Dad, but my stomach flipped over again, spinning me back around to the toilet.

After the final contents of my stomach came up, I laid down on the bathroom floor, my check against the cool tile when my house half exploded with the sound of my father's voice.

"That little shit! I'll kill him!" Dad screamed.

I couldn't make out Mom's words, but her voice was more animated than I remembered hearing from her in a long time. I caught a few phrases like *keeping it quiet…won't do anyone any good…the more fuss you make the bigger deal it will become…trying to pass a law, and can't afford any press…*

I wasn't fooled. It wasn't going to blow over.

That was the one and only time my father ever hit me.

He stomped up the stairs, but I was too nauseated to care. I kept my face pressed into the floor.

"Delia, come out here right now!" Dad wasn't like that often—out of control angry. I wanted no part of it. I lay silent on the floor, my eyes closed as tightly as I could, wishing him away.

In seconds my bathroom door flew open. Dad grabbed me by the arm, jerked me to standing and backhanded the side of my face so hard I nearly passed out.

I stayed home until the swelling went down. Wore a T-shirt to cover the bruises on my arm.

I never told a soul. Especially not Tobin. There was *nothing* that would've stopped him from going to jail for assaulting my dad if he knew.

- - -

What a mess. I found out we were moving, then I found out I was pregnant, and before Tobin or I had time to process, I was gone. Dad whirl-winded me through an abortion, and Tobin and I forgot how to talk to each other. At least I understand that he was scared, like me.

It just wasn't what I expected from Tobin—he seemed invincible. We could have handled the move. We could have handled the pregnancy. But both in such a short amount of time, and us not appreciating what we had in the other—that was our downfall.

I don't even try to hold in my smile. Second chances are beautiful things.

The trail ends on my lawn, and I'm geared up and ready to face Dad, but see Weston. He's in my driveway pulling his golf clubs from the garage.

"Hey." I jog toward him. "I wanna talk." And hope that he'll listen.

26

Tobin

I squint as the sun streams in through the single window of the cabin. I can't see a damn thing, but I don't even have to feel next to me—I know she's gone. The warmth that *is* Delia is not here. She said she'd stay. It feels like some warped form of payback.

"I can't give you the life that you are used to, Delia," I'd told her last night.

"Thank God," she laughed.

I thought she meant it. But maybe she was having second thoughts. Maybe a life of fancy homes and personal chefs and a closet full of expensive clothes wasn't something she was willing to let go of. Nice of her to fill me in.

I roll the sleeping bag back up, toss it haphazardly into the corner, and grab my keys. I don't care if Mr. Gentry is home. I don't care if Ralph Lauren answers the door. I'm going over there to confront her.

The entire drive should take about ten minutes, and it may have, but it feels like ten years. I can hear the blood whooshing in my ears, my anger percolating with each passing minute. When I drive up to the Gentry estate, I pull right into the driveway. Screw the oil leak, I don't care anymore. I take the front steps two at a time. I'm all ready to knock, but the front door is open. Through the hurricane screen, I can see Delia there. *In Ralph Lauren's arms.*

I don't know what I expected, but honestly, it wasn't this.

I start to turn away, but I hear her call me. I don't stop until I am at the door to my truck.

"Tobin, what are you doing?" She jogs up behind me. "I know you heard me. Why did you walk away?"

"I don't know, Delia. Let me think. Maybe because you let me hold you all night and now you're right back in his arms. So last night was what? Just sympathy about Eamon? Next time, save yourself the trouble." I climb into my truck and slam the door.

"Tobin LeJeune, you ass! We spent a year misunderstanding each other and you're just going to go and mess everything up again?" She stomps her foot and crosses her arms. I can't help but smile. As soon as I do, she leans into the window and kisses my shoulder.

Her lips are like magic, instantly, I feel the anger slip away.

"So, what's going on then?" I ask. "Why did you leave? I've waited too long to wake up next to you again."

"I couldn't stay. Not until I ended things with Weston the right way. If there is a *right* way," she says. "He's just passing through on his way to Tennessee, but I broke up with him. I mean, I broke up with him before, but I think I made it okay this time. He's heading out. What you saw was goodbye. That's it."

"Your dad is not going to be happy about this," I say.

"Do you really care about Randy Gentry's happiness?" she asks, with the beginnings of a smile.

"I care about yours," I say. I touch her chin with my thumb. I want to tell her not to, but maybe things have gone on like this for too long.

"Then go. I'm ready to take him on."

"D, at least let me be there for that."

She shakes her head. "I really need to do this on my own, Tobin. I gave up everything that I loved because he said so, and I hate myself for it. It's time for me to stand up to him."

"I love you, Delia Gentry," I say.

A small smile creeps across her tan face.

"Well, Tobin LeJeune, that's convenient, because I never stopped loving you."

I tangle my hand into the hair at the nape of her neck and pull her lips toward mine.

"Lets not adding insult to injury." She does a half-glance to where polo-boy stands on the porch. "Come back after dinner, okay?" she says. "That is, if I'm worth it." She winks at me as I pull out of the driveway.

She's a lot tougher than she gives herself credit for. Not many people would survive living with her father. All I can do for her right now is pray she knows how strong she is when she tells her daddy she isn't leaving with him.

That man tried to scare the hell out of me more than once.

⌬

"I saw Delia's old man outside of the welding shop today. What was up with that?" Eamon asked me. Eamon was laying low near the front of the small mudboat, while I held the spot light over his shoulder.

"There's one to your right," I said. I pointed to the large pig frog. Eamon swiped at it and it made a loud, pig-like grunt before he palmed it and shoved it into the sack. We had already caught a couple of dozen in the hour we'd been out on the water.

"Same old shit. Wants me to stay away from his daughter. He's heading back to Washington next week, so you know, he needs to give me the usual warning. I think he's hoping someday it'll actually stick."

"She's hot, bro, don't get me wrong. But is she

worth this total pain in the ass that her dad has become? I mean, waiting for you outside of work?" He shook his head. Eamon would never end up in a situation like this, because he would never be in a relationship long enough.

"She's worth it." I kept it short.

"Here finish this," he said. He passed me what was left of a joint. I flicked it into the river. Eamon watched it float away in the brown water and frowned.

"Still going soft on me, I see," he said. "She must be killer in the sack, huh?"

"Eamon, don't make me have to kick your ass," I said.

He let out a loud laugh and clapped his hands on his knees.

"I'm messing with you. You say she's worth it, I believe you. Now let's get home and fry these suckers up," he said.

I miss him.

HOPE

Hope is a ledge
A walkway
A cliff
To really use it, you have to leap off
But that takes faith

Faith that the person you're leaping for
Will catch you
Because they want to
Because the feel of you slamming into their arms
Is worth everything

For them
For you
Forever

27

Delia

Damn Tobin. How many times will I have said that by the time I get this mess straightened out? This time I say it to myself with a smile. Tobin is who he is. Impulsive. Protective. Stubborn. Amazing.

Weston drives away, and I take a look down at my dirty feet, ragged shorts, and stained tank. Every piece of the mess that I am makes me smile. And nothing's keeping me from waking up next to Tobin tomorrow.

Weston's hurt, and I hurt, too. He just wasn't right. At least I got to tell him why. About who I am, and about how he helped me when I needed it most. There was no way to keep telling Weston I wasn't leaving him for Tobin, because I spent last night in his arms.

It feels like I haven't slept in days, and I guess I really haven't. The emotional stress of Eamon, Tobin, Weston…it's all starting to crash down around me.

I turn toward the house, my stomach a mess of knots, and I just hope that it's early enough to give me some time to gather my thoughts.

As I move through the kitchen, I see Mom in her favorite lounge chair in our screened porch with a drink in her hand. Her laptop is open next to her. She isn't looking at it, though, she's just staring out into the trees.

"Mom?" I sit down, wondering how to even begin to tell her what I want to do. Wonder if I know what I want to do, and wonder if there's any way to make it happen and still be speaking with my parents.

"Was I a good Mom to you?" she asks without moving.

"I...of course. Don't be silly." Is what I say, but the truth is, I don't know. I'd never even thought of it much before. We've always seemed like the two women living in the shadow of my father. I know that things will be different now for me, but she'll still be with him. I can't imagine a universe in which my mother walks out on my father.

"I think I should have stood up for you more," she says.

Yes, I want to scream. But instead, I'm still not sure what to say to her. I just want peace. With everyone. She and Dad already fight too much; I didn't ever want to make it worse. It never occurred to me to ask Mom for help against Dad. Neither of us would be able to sway him, I knew that.

"You were happy here. With Tobin I mean." She sighs. "Before we moved to D.C."

I'm shaky again at the mention of his name. Tobin was always a subject we avoided in our house.

"Yes. I mean, it was rough for us knowing we had the big decision to make about the baby." I can't believe I just said that out loud. "And then even harder when Dad was over-stressed and then Tobin and I didn't know what to say to each other anymore." What else am I supposed to say?

"I should have stood up for you more." She repeats. "I'm sorry, Delia." She reaches over and pats my hand. Something she'd do to appease my father or anyone else. I think it's all so automatic for her now that she doesn't give it a second thought.

"I just…" I still don't know how to explain. "I just want to feel like I own my decisions."

Her bright blue eyes find mine. There is a spark behind them. Something real.

"That, Delia, is an excellent place to start."

This is more attention than I've gotten from my mom in a long time. It makes me sad, but also make me realize that I don't need her. I can do things on my own. Have been doing things on my own without fully realizing it. "I love you, Mom."

She relaxes back into her chair and takes another sip of her drink. Her email pings. She pats my hand. "Love you, too, sweetie." But she's half into email already.

Wow.

Okay.

The sad thing is that probably nothing much will change between us. I guess that's okay. It is what it is.

Dad's heavy footsteps come down the stairs, so I stand and move into the kitchen, knowing he'll have something to say to me about how I wasn't home all night. Again.

He glances up when I come into sight. "You had a late night last night. I'm not going to be cleaning up any more of your messes, am I?" There's an edge of anger to his voice, but it's quiet, controlled. Maybe he's just tired.

And is that how he sees my abortion? A mess? I mean, it was a mess, but it was so much more than that. It's something I'll always carry with me.

His large hand reaches toward the closet door and he stand there for a moment, maybe trying to remember what he brought that still needs to be packed.

"Celebration for Eamon," I say. "That's where I was."

"And Weston?" His face is harder, and so is his voice.

This is the point where I always back down. Walk away. Especially after the bathroom incident.

I'm shaking all over because I'm about to give him the truth. All of it. "I didn't love Weston the same way he loved me. It wasn't fair to him."

Dad's hard laugh sounds more like a growl. "So,

when you broke his heart, you were really doing him a *favor?* Is that what you want me to believe? Don't think I don't know what happens in my house!"

Dad's more than angry, he's pissed over Weston— throwing one of his favorite lines at me. I'm sure it'll damage the relationship with Weston's dad. But I'm hoping that after this morning, Weston will be okay. Maybe it won't be as bad as Dad thinks.

"Umm…not right now, no. But in ten years from now both Weston and I will be glad we separated now rather than later. So, yes." I'm not sure why I'm trying to reason with Dad when there's no way he wants to reason with me.

"Dammit, Delia!" His fists clench up. "You can't even see a good thing when you've got it! I don't know what to do with you!"

His yell rings between us for a moment, and then silence just hangs.

"Maybe I'm not your problem anymore." But my voice is so quiet that I have no idea if he heard or not.

I can feel Dad's anger simmering, just waiting to really let loose. I try not to visibly shake.

"Delia." His eyes finally meet mine for real, and I suddenly wish he was half dismissing me like he did earlier.

"I'm going to stay here for a while," I say. "In Crawford."

His whole face relaxes, a reaction I don't understand, and one that I definitely didn't expect.

"No you're not, Delia. Go pack whatever you need. I have a plane scheduled to meet us in an hour." He doesn't even give me a second glance, just turns and continues to check tags on suitcases and zippers. Doesn't think for a second that I'll go against him.

"An hour?" My heart starts thrumming. "I thought we were here until tonight. What about Mom's car. We drove, and—"

"I changed it. You're not acting like yourself." He scoots one bag closer to the door and begins looking over the next.

I'm acting more like myself than I have in over a year. "I'm staying, Dad." I say it with way more resolve than I feel.

"Delia." He sighs as he drops his suitcase and wipes his forehead with another handkerchief. "I don't have time for your teenage ridiculousness. Please go get dressed in something decent, pull up your hair, pack your bags so we can get out of this place and go home."

I can barely breathe, but I owe it to Tobin to fight for him. And more than that, I owe it to myself. "This *is* home."

Dad's jaw tightens.

Maybe if I plead with him, like I used to do for shoes and fundraiser outfits. "I don't want to fight with you

Daddy, but this is my home, and I want to stay here for a while."

"Delia, I'm not messing around."

"Neither am I." I cross my arms and try to keep my voice calm. "You're not as big of a big-shot as you think you are, Dad. No one will notice if I disappear for a while. You can play on the angle of me staying in our hometown as they mourn the loss of one of their young men. Or you can say nothing."

"Get upstairs, get dressed, and *get in the car*!" He means to be obeyed. Dad isn't used to anyone telling him no.

"I can't." It comes out in a squeak.

"Delia." Dad's fury is in his tightened jaw, clenched fists, hard breathing. He takes a step toward me, and I know he's going to hit me. I know it.

I start to cower away, but stop. If I stand here, the worst that'll happen is I get a black eye. But if I continue to let him bully me, I'll never be free. I'll never have Tobin. I'll never have any peace of mind. "Go ahead." I step toward him.

Dad pauses, his eyes hard on me. His shoulder and arm twitching, ready to strike.

I want to threaten him. Tell him that if he touches me, I'll turn him in. I want to threaten to work for the democrats. Donate time to Planned Parenthood.

But I don't.

I just stand.

Dad turns twenty shades of purple. The silence is thicker than the hot, damp, air. But I'm not standing down. Not on this. My life is spread out before me and he's not going to take it. I can't let him. Hot tears start to come down my face, but my determination hasn't wavered. I'm doing it. I'm worth this. *Enough.*

Mom walks in from the kitchen, laptop under her arm and dressed for travel—plain skirt, lower heels and a blouse. She pats Dad on the shoulder without making eye contact with either of us. "Let her stay." I wait for a second glance back from Mom, but she continues her walk toward the car. Maybe she's okay with what I'm doing…maybe she's not. Maybe she's just trying to keep me from the same fate as her.

I know I need to give him an easy way out. "Please, Dad. I'm asking to stay in the town you raised me in. Surely if I'm needed here you can say something about that. Probably people won't even ask. They know I've graduated."

I'm going to have to actually start responding to texts from friends so they know I won't be home. And I'll miss some of them, but not all. Not the way I'd miss my friends from here. I'm no longer running from these people or this place, because I'm not long running from Tobin.

He stares at the door that Mom walked through.

His eyes don't pass back toward me. "We expect you to be in college in the fall like we planned." He snatches his suitcase and heads for the door without another word.

"Love you, Dad."

The door slams behind him, and my legs give out as I slide to the floor.

I did it.

28

Tobin

"Tobin, can you come see?" Mom calls from the front porch.

The screen door squeaks as I fling it open. She's sitting in her rocking chair with a book on her lap. She's dressed in *actual* clothes for the first time since the funeral, and everything about the scene looks closer to normal than it has in a while.

"What's up, Mama?" I say. I kiss the top of her head, and catch the soft, familiar scent. She's wearing perfume again, too. It smells like my childhood. Running into her arms after Eamon and I had been out all day causing trouble.

"I know things haven't been easy on you, Tobin. I know I put a lot on you when it all first happened. I just want you to know that I love you, too. That you were both my favorite sons."

I smile. She hasn't said that in a long time, but when Eamon and I were younger, she'd say it all the time. We were always in competition, always wanting to one up the other, even when it came to her love, so Mama always called us both her favorite sons.

"I know, Mama."

"You boys were so close. And so alike. But in other ways, so different, Tobin. Your *hearts* were different."

"Where you going with this?" I ask.

"You *are* enough, Tobin. I know you've been trying to stay away and give her some time, but you go and get that girl, and you don't let her go this time. If losing your brother has taught me anything, it's to hold the ones that I love closer than ever. You best do the same, son."

It's then that my mind goes to the ring that I threw out into the darkness when I let go of Delia once and for all, or so I thought. There's no way to find it now. Part of me feels like a huge asshole for throwing it away, but the other part knows that it was for the best.

If Delia and I are ever going to stand a chance, we need a fresh start. Someday, maybe there will be another ring.

One that's more like she deserves. One not tainted by so much hurt.

One that lasts forever.

29

Delia

I can't remember the last time I was really, truly alone.

It feels good. Better than good.

I lie on the dock in the last bits of sunset and pull my knees up as I watch the sky slowly turn into darker shades of blue.

There's footsteps on the dock, and I don't have to move to know its Tobin. After all this time, so many things haven't changed at all. I love everything familiar.

"I still have a lot to figure out," I say without moving.

He sits next to me, pulling his knees up and resting his elbows there. I love Tobin's profile. I love that he's here next to me.

"Don't we all."

"My parents are gone," I say.

"How long are you staying then?" He's asking a lot more than my travel plans.

"I don't plan on going anywhere." I reach my hand out to take his as I sit up, letting my body touch his side.

Tobin feels like everything. My past. My future. My

home. We're not getting a redo, more like re-start, and it'll take some time, but I don't think either of use will take the other for granted. Not this time.

His arm comes around me and the silence wraps us up and relaxes me into his side. Who knew it would be Eamon who would bring us together in the end.

"What do you miss most about him?" I ask.

"Who, Eamon?" Tobin says, running his hand across his stubbly cheek. "Jesus, D, so many things. Every single day it's something new. I miss everything about him. I even miss him giving me so much shit."

I laugh. "I miss how he could never call me by my first name. Ever! It was always Miss Priss, or Gentry. I used to pretend that it annoyed me, but I really did love that. I loved him." I can feel the tightness in my throat building and I almost wish I never brought it up, but being next to Tobin makes it okay.

"He loved you too," Tobin says. His eyes are soft and I can tell that some of the hurt in him is healing.

"I'm glad you're here."

His fingers slide through mine as he squeezes my hand. "Glad doesn't begin to cover it, Delia." He leans toward me until our foreheads touch.

I blink a few times, trying to keep my tears away.

His hand reaches across and touches my cheek,

sliding back until his fingers are wound in my hair, and his hand rests on the back of my neck sending a wash of emotions through me so powerful it takes my breath away. It's all here. All of it. All of him. And me. And everything we are together.

I want to say something. To tell him how I love him, how I can't believe we made it back here, but I know by the way he's touching me that I don't have to.

"My heart for yours," he offers.

"Deal."

And just after the very last pieces of the sun disappear, Tobin's lips touch mine in the beginning and ending and middle of everything we had and will have. Together.

TOGETHER

There were friends
Who traded
Shirts for shirts
Hands for hands
Lies for lies
Mistakes for more

When white turned black
And black turned grey

It changed

Truths for truths
Hearts for hearts
Souls for souls
Lives for life

And we're really happy.

ACKNOWLEDGEMENTS

First of all – Stephanie Campbell is a rockstar. She doesn't sleep. I'd send her the doc, and she'd work her a** off on it. I'd check my email one last time before going to sleep, and I'd have more writing from her. She lives FOUR time zones ahead of me. It was a blast to do this project together, and I know we'll make time to do one again.

For my EVER patient husband, Mike, for listening to my clacking while he watches his "man shows." If the clacking of computer keys slows down, it means that I'm about to make fun of something that happened on-screen, and he's pretty awesome about that, too.

My kids are amazing, and have learned to just laugh when I say - *just a sec!* Because we all know it'll take me longer than that.

Steph and I have some of the best author friends in the UNIVERSE – so thanks a TON for your unwavering support.

–Jolene

Ditto to what Jo said about us having the absolute biggest supporters and friends in the author world. We are so lucky! You know who you are.

For my husband Chris, and my darling kiddos- Hailey, Liam, Finnian and Britta for tolerating me even though I don't ever sleep- and often act like it.

Thanks to Jo for being so willing to dive right into yet another project when she always has eleventy-billion other things in the works. Writing with you was a joy!

To Natasha Angelino and Shellie Fernandez. You have been in my life since I was ten years old, and I never would have made it back to writing after the ordeal with B if it weren't for your unwavering support every single day. I love you both so much.

And,

Thanks to Michael LeJeune for letting me borrow your last name. ☺

-Steph

About the Authors

Jolene Perry grew up in Alaska, ended up back in Wasilla after college with her husband and two children. She plays the guitar, sings when forced, and used her degree in Political Science and French to teach math. She now writes.

Also by Jolene - NIGHT SKY, KNEE DEEP, SPILL OVER, DIZZY (with Nyrae Dawn), 10 WEEKS, INSIGHT, FALLING. She has many more projects on the way.

You can find her at @jolenebperry, on her personal blog jolenesbeenwriting.blogspot.com, as well as her author site jolenebperry.com

Steph Campbell grew up in Southern California, but now calls Southwest Louisiana home. She has one husband, four children and a serious nail polish obsession. Also by Steph are the YA novel's GROUNDING QUINN, DELICATE, BEAUTIFUL THINGS NEVER LAST (2013). LENGTHS and A TOAST TO THE GOOD TIMES, both written with Liz Reinhardt.

You can find her on twitter at @stephcampbell_ and her blog: stephcampbell.blogspot.com.